Barnsley Libraries

CLASH OF HEARTS

When Albany's father is severely injured in the bomb disaster that kills her mother, Albany abandons her career as a physiotherapist in order to care for him. They rent a cottage on a Dorset estate from the owner, Olivia Blaire, and hope to start life afresh. Albany makes friends with the handsome Dr Planter, and he is able to give her some of his private patients. But when she meets Olivia's arrogant stepson, Sebastian, Albany's dreams are shattered.

Books by Stella Ross
in the Linford Romance Library:

SHADOW OF THE PAST
PAIN OF BETRAYAL
YESTERDAY'S LOVE
SEA SPELL

STELLA ROSS

CLASH OF HEARTS

Complete and Unabridged

LINFORD
Leicester

First published in Great Britain in 1989 by
Robert Hale Limited
London

First Linford Edition
published 1999
by arrangement with
Robert Hale Limited
London

British Library CIP Data

Ross, Stella
 Clash of hearts.—Large print ed.—
Linford roamance library
 1. Large type books
 2. Large type books
 I. Title
 823.9′14 [F]

 ISBN 0–7089–5583–5

Published by
F. A. Thorpe (Publishing) Ltd.
Anstey, Leicestershire

Set by Words & Graphics Ltd.
Anstey, Leicestershire
Printed and bound in Great Britain by
T. J. International Ltd., Padstow, Cornwall

This book is printed on acid-free paper

1

'Nearly there now,' Albany told her father, 'just round this next corner.'

She followed the line of the hedge tightly, remembering its sharpness from her last visit and guiding her car expertly round the bend.

Almost at once the countryside opened up and clusters of small, white cottages appeared, erupting like mushrooms on a warm wet night among the smooth, rounded Dorsetshire hills.

Not too far in the distance she could make out the tall, old-stone walls that surrounded Blaire Manor; its attractive Jacobean chimneys just visible as dark, straight lines amidst the lush foliage of chestnuts, limes and plane trees that bounded the property.

A pair of wide, ornamental gates slipped into sight before they had driven much further and, behind them, Drive

Cottage with its latticed windows set in centuries-old limestone reared into view. The sight, for some unknown reason, slightly disturbed her as it had done before. She shrugged the feeling away quickly, bringing her silver Fiesta to a halt in front of the drive gates, and studying her father as he devoured his first glimpse of their new home.

'Well, what do you think of it?' Her tone was anxious and she tried to cover it with a light laugh. 'It looked a bit like Bleak House in the rain the other day, but I must say it looks more pleasant in the sunshine.'

For a moment Darrel Edmunds showed the first sign of pleasure since the tragic accident six months ago that had robbed him of his wife, and left him devoid of all precious movement below the waist.

'Very nice,' he said with a nod, 'if a trifle austere. But I'm still not clear how you managed to find it, or how you inveigled the owner into letting us rent it?'

She pretended to grow impatient. 'I explained everything to you a week ago. You probably weren't taking the trouble to listen.'

He looked so lost and unhappy trying to bring the occasion back to mind that, not for the first time, she felt her heart go out to him. Six months ago he had been a vital, active person. Now, due to a terrorist bomb that had exploded in the Spanish town where he'd been holidaying with his wife, he'd been left partially paralysed and seemed to have difficulty recalling small events.

She watched him give a frown of recollection. 'I seem to remember you saying something about an old schoolfriend . . .'

She put him in the picture for the fifth time.

'That's right — Rachel Robinson. The tubby old thing turned up in the physiotherapy department out of the blue. It gave me the shock of my life. I hadn't seen her for thirteen years — since we were both fifteen. I must say she looked almost middle-aged. I hope she didn't think the same about me!'

She stole a small, vain look in the driving mirror to reassure herself. The face that stared back was definitely not middle-aged, nor was it short of attraction. Long, fair hair that she'd piled casually on top, left curling tendrils trailing softly against her cheeks. Her face was heart-shaped with regular features. Wide-apart blue eyes, besides holding an alert, intelligent gaze, also had a slightly authoritative appearance.

'Anyway,' she went on, 'Rachel coming to the clinic turned out to be a godsend. We went over to the canteen for coffee after I'd treated her. There, in the course of swapping information, I found out she'd married someone quite well off. According to her, her husband's only a few steps away from a title, would you believe?' She stopped, finding the thought of Rachel in an ermine cape and tiara almost too foolish to contemplate.

'Well, as I was saying, Rachel's aristocratic husband, Robert, has an aunt by marriage who owns Blaire Manor — or rather her step-son does, but he's out of the country at the moment, and according to Rachel, seems set to stay there. So when I started to tell her I was looking for somewhere peaceful for us to live while you convalesced, she came up with the idea that the Manor's west lodge might suit us admirably. And she thought it was already vacant. Naturally I jumped at it at once and drove down to see Mrs Blaire, who seemed to be a nice enough person. She said that since the place was fully furnished and gathering dust she could think of no good reason why we shouldn't have it at a reasonable rent for as long as we liked. So I promptly offered to give her a spot of free treatment for a stiff shoulder that's been worrying her. Then, a few days ago, I signed an agreement and here we are.'

She glanced sideways at him, secretly grieving at how much he had aged. He was only fifty-six, but over the last six months his hair had grown almost white.

He observed her scrutiny and touched her arm lightly.

'Stop feeling so sorry for me. I should have refused to let you go on with this silly idea. You're far too young to take on the responsibility of an invalid. I should have put myself into a home.'

'Don't be ridiculous! Who do you think would have you? You're far too independent to be stuck in a home. They don't cater for active people.'

He gave a bitter laugh. 'Active did you say? I'll never walk again and you know it.'

'All right,' she agreed. 'But your mind is still active, though you pretend to be forgetful. There are lots of desk jobs you can do. Anyway, we're not thinking about work until you've recovered from that last operation.'

'And what about you?' he asked gruffly. 'How do you expect to keep yourself? You've given up a promising and rewarding career to take care of me!'

She laughed. 'Don't you believe it. You won't need looking after twenty four hours a day. In fact you've a rude awakening coming. You're going to have to fend for yourself while I'm out treating a few private patients. One of the first things I shall do after we've settled in is to make myself known to the local doctor for possible referrals. That should keep me in clothes and food and other refinements.'

He shook his head. 'You know I didn't mean money-wise. I meant friends, well-loved surroundings, everything you'd built up for yourself.'

She told a small lie. 'I'd grown tired of the clinic and I'm quite looking forward to a change.'

She got out quickly before he could say any more and opened the heavy gates. Then she slid back in and gave him a warm smile.

'Welcome home! Let's cut the heart-to-hearts and have a look at our new abode.'

It was about fifty yards from the gates to where the lodge named Drive Cottage lay. A garage had been added at the side and a short privet hedge surrounded the small garden. As Albany looked up at the windows she felt the same sensation of unease that she had experienced twice before. This time she tried to examine it rationally.

She had never set eyes on the place until she had gone there on Rachel's recommendation two weeks before. Most of her life had been spent in Oxfordshire. There was just a slight possibility that she might have driven past at some time, but she had no recollection of having met anyone who had ever lived there.

The feeling vanished almost as quickly as it had come. Her father's wheelchair was folded up in the boot and she fetched it for him. After helping him in, she took out the key and opened the front door.

Inside, everything had been freshly polished and hoovered since her last visit. Roses from the Manor gardens had been placed in huge bowls on the wide, attractive window sills. Sunlight streamed in through diamond-shaped panes. She looked round, slightly relieved at the happy transformation.

Her father's examination of the cottage was confined of necessity to the ground floor. She was glad to see interest returning to his gaze as he wheeled himself slowly around.

'I'll ask Mrs Blaire if she's averse to a few small alterations being made — such as ramps for the wheelchair,' she volunteered.

He nodded, thinking about something else.

'How long did you say it's been since the place has been lived in?' He noticed the roses. 'It seems someone has very kindly gone out of their way to make us feel at home.'

Albany agreed. 'I told you, Mrs Blaire seemed quite a pleasant person, if a bit on the talkative side. From what she told me I gather the place has been empty for about a year. But Mrs Blaire's only lived at the Manor for half that time: she moved in while her step-son was still abroad.'

Darrel Edmunds looked slightly worried.

'Do I recall you saying she's not the true owner?'

'So Rachel said. It belongs to her step-son.'

'Then what authority has she to draw up an agreement?'

Albany shrugged. 'Maybe he's given her power of attorney?'

Darrel wheeled himself around, studying the furniture pensively. 'I sincerely hope so.'

She gave a laugh. 'Stop looking so anxious, the contract is perfectly valid. It's been drawn up by a firm of solicitors. I'll show it you later.'

She watched as he wheeled himself

over to the window to look out at the view. While he was there she opened a door leading off from the sitting room that had once been a morning room. It had now been turned into a downstairs bedroom.

Darrel became interested again. 'I presume that one's mine?'

'Yes,' she said. 'What do you think? I suggested it to Mrs Blaire since there's a downstairs loo right next door as well as a shower.' She slipped past him to open the adjoining door. 'Ah, yes — she's had the shower seat fitted. I wondered if she'd remember. She's a bit of a feather-brained person.'

While he was growing accustomed to the downstairs she went up to examine the room she'd chosen for herself the last time she was there. It was the first bedroom at the top of the stairs. As she stood in the doorway a chill feeling came over her. The words of an old French nursery rhyme suddenly flew into her head: *Au clair de la lune, mon ami Pierrot . . .*

11

She gave a little shudder.

After she'd returned downstairs they examined the well-equipped kitchen together. Later Albany fetched a box of groceries from the car.

'Perhaps you'd like to come up with me this afternoon to meet Mrs Blaire and let her know we've arrived?'

'No.' Darrel Edmunds shook his head firmly. 'I'll stay here and get my bearings for a few days first.'

She smiled at him with understanding. 'You're doing fine, Dad! Take as long as you like. Just let me know when you're ready and I'll give you a lift up in the car. It's a hefty walk till you get more strength in your arms.'

★ ★ ★

The first week after their arrival passed quickly. On the fifth day Darrel Edmunds accepted Albany's offer of a lift up to the Manor. He had grown weary of sitting in the cottage on his own, and had begun to take an interest in exploring his immediate surroundings.

It was what Albany had prayed for. At last, after six months of pain and grieving, he was beginning to crawl out of his tight shell and show the desire to live again.

Mrs Blaire seemed pleased to receive them both, and they sat out on the wide patio near the rose garden in the June sunshine sipping cool drinks.

She was very well dressed and made-up and her fingers dripped with large-stoned rings. She had a stagey, artificial way of talking.

'I'm so glad you and Albany have taken over Drive Cottage. I do hope we shall all be good friends. I often find the Manor almost unbearably lonely. Sebastian, my step-son, keeps so few staff. As I mentioned to Albany, my husband has been dead for eighteen months. And Sebastian is in Africa — or he was the last time I heard from him.'

'I understand you've only lived at

Blaire Manor for the past six months?'

'That's true, Mr Edmunds — or may I call you Darrel? My name is Olivia. It's a pure twist of fate that our surname happens to be the same as this house. Sebastian bought it for himself about two years ago. His father and I were still living in the Lake District at the time.' She played with her rings sadly. 'After his father's death I lived alone for a year. But the fact was I found I couldn't go on affording the upkeep. So I wrote to Sebastian and told him, and he suggested I sold Lakeview and came down here to keep an eye on his house. It was such a shame to have somewhere as beautiful as this standing idle while he roamed the world.'

'What a shame for you your son can't be home more often,' Albany said. 'Is it his work that takes him abroad?'

Mrs Blaire gave a frown of displeasure.

'Oh, no, Sebastian doesn't need to work. He's only thirty but he's been extremely lucky for such a young man.

He inherited a great deal of money on the death of his uncle.' Her mouth turned down. 'Such a pity in some ways because I think inherited wealth can be very harmful to character. Not that I'm over-familiar with Sebastian's character.' She gave a shrug, examining a pink, well manicured nail. 'You see, unfortunately my husband's son is still almost a stranger to me. He was already very grown-up when I married his father. I don't think he's ever really approved of me. I must be so different from his mother.'

'All the same it was very kind of him to suggest you moved in here in his absence.'

'Oh yes, extremely kind.' Olivia Blaire's manner changed. 'My dear Albany, you mustn't run away with the idea that I'm not grateful to my step-son — or that I'm making him out to be cold or unusual. He's really very, very kind, and extraordinarily handsome. Just like his dear father. I have a photograph of the two of them together that I always carry about with me.' She dug around with her pointed nails inside her handbag until she drew out a crumpled snapshot. 'Here it is,' she said proudly. 'It was taken in our garden at Lakeview. It's several years old, but it's still a very good likeness, I'm sure.'

Albany studied the photograph closely. It showed father and son standing next to an old fashioned sundial. The younger person was tall and slim and dwarfed the older man by almost a foot. It was true, as Mrs Blaire had said, her step-son was enormously good looking. He was dark haired and dark eyed with a steady gaze. Without knowing why, Albany came to the conclusion that he was probably arrogant, too. Perhaps the thought arose because he was rich enough to buy a place like Blaire Manor and then spend so little time there.

She handed the snap-shot back. 'You're right,' she said, without really meaning it. 'He looks extremely kind.'

'Oh, he is, he is,' Olivia Blaire said in her stagey voice. 'And so generous, too, to let me stay here.' Then her rather close-together eyes grew narrow. 'But then, of course, he can so easily afford it.'

Albany looked down at her watch. 'I hope you'll both excuse me if I dash off now. I think I mentioned that I've an appointment to see Doctor Planter at five. I don't want to be late.'

'I must leave, too,' Darrel Edmunds said hurriedly. He gave his daughter a swift smile. 'But you don't have to ferry me home. I shall test my strength and roll gently back under my own steam.'

'Oh, must you both leave so soon?' Mrs Blaire said, sounding disappointed. 'Oh well — if you must, you must. However, I shall always be glad to see either of you whenever you care to come up. Perhaps you'd like to borrow some books, Darrel? And maybe you'll allow me to call at the cottage occasionally when I'm passing?'

Darrel gave his daughter the tiniest of warning glances which Albany immediately picked up and deciphered. She could tell her father didn't care very much for Olivia Blaire.

She thought of a quick excuse. 'I hope to start work shortly. And father doesn't always sleep well at night so I encourage him to lie down when he feels like it during the day to allow his last operation to mend.'

Olivia seemed to get the message.

'Oh, there's no need to explain. I should always ring beforehand, in any case. But it mustn't stop either of you from coming up to see me whenever you want. I believe we agreed that the rent should be paid weekly in cash, didn't we?'

In the end they were able to take their leave of her. As Albany kissed her father goodbye and got in her car she gave a wry smile.

'Sorry if she frightened you off. I didn't realise she was quite such an ogress.'

He nodded. 'I can understand why her step-son extends his absences.'

Albany reminded him: 'It was still kind of her to let us have the cottage, though. Even though you say the rent's a bit steep.'

'That's so. But you must let me have sight of that agreement some time. I'm still interested to know what right she has to let her step-son's property.'

'I'll let you have it this evening,' she promised, switching on the engine. 'I must go now. Take care going home. Wish me luck!'

He gave her a wave, then began to wheel himself gently along the drive towards the cottage, conscious of the fact that Olivia Blaire was keeping tabs on him from behind the heavy curtains of the Manor sitting room.

★ ★ ★

Albany's interview with Doctor Miles Planter turned out to be a much easier ordeal than she had dared to hope. He was young, in his early thirties, fair haired and attractively tanned.

He made it clear he was taken with her. His bold eyes took in every small detail, from the shapeliness of her slender knees crossed neatly over each other in the opposite chair, to the fine, closely textured bloom of her complexion, which he could see needed no artificial aids to beauty other than the faintest touch of eye-liner and a trace of lipstick.

He listened attentively as she outlined her father's plight before going on to tell him of her own aspirations in the direction of private patients.

'I presume you have all the necessary qualifications?' he asked.

'I'd hardly be here taking up your valuable time if I hadn't,' she replied, raising a winged eyebrow. 'I've been a practising physiotherapist for several years now. My clinic was attached to the same hospital my father was in. We've moved down here to give us both a new start.'

He smiled. 'I'm sorry. But I'm flattered you consider my time valuable.' He gave a glance at his watch. 'It *is*. My partner is taking over surgery this evening while I put in a spot of sailing. It's my one and only vice.' His frank gaze studied her figure with interest again. 'Well, nearly,' he added.

She stood up, conscious of the fact that she'd made a conquest and feeling rather proud of herself.

'Then I can bank on your help, Doctor Planter? That's very kind of you. Naturally, I don't want to be kept *too* busy. My father will need my companionship and help for some time yet.'

'The name's Miles,' he said as he showed her out. 'And you say you live at Drive Cottage? That's one of the lodges at Blaire Manor, isn't it?'

She nodded. 'Yes, the west one.'

He looked suddenly thoughtful. 'It's been empty for some time now, ever since . . . ' he broke off.

'You were saying?' she prompted curiously.

His smile reappeared. 'Oh, nothing.' He put out his hand and took hers in a firm grip. 'Good evening, Miss Edmunds — Albany! What a pretty name. I'll be in touch as soon as I have a patient for you. And perhaps you'd ring reception tomorrow and make an appointment for me to see your father.'

She smiled back. 'I'll definitely do that. And thank you very much, Doctor Planter.'

He waved a reproving finger at her. 'Ah — ah — ah!'

'Miles,' she amended, feeling a slight ripple of pleasure.

2

Albany's friendship with Miles Planter blossomed over the next month, though she kept any attempts he made at romantic overtures well at bay. She had no intention of being swept off her feet within so short a while of moving to Dorset. He was good company, full of fun, intelligent and pleasant. But Albany had been infatuated enough times in her twenty-eight years to recognise that what she had sometimes mistaken for love could be very short-lasting. And, anyway, from information she'd picked up, Miles Planter seemed to have enough female company to keep him adequately occupied without her adding to it.

All the same, she had to admit to herself that she enjoyed chatting to him on the phone whenever he rang to let her know he was sending one of his patients her way. And she found pleasure in their frequent meetings. So it was understandable that when one day he casually invited her to go sailing with him, she dropped her guard and found herself accepting.

When she mentioned it to her father he only half encouraged the outing.

'You spend too much time with older folk. It'll do you good to get some salt air in your lungs. But watch yourself,' he warned, 'that young fellow's got an eye for the girls, as I expect you've already found out. Don't let yourself get silly over him.'

She raised her eyebrows. 'You say that, yet you realise I'll be out at sea alone with him. It's a long swim home if he says he's run out of diesel fuel!'

Her father smiled. 'I expect you can trust him. He's got too much to lose if he forces his attentions on someone who doesn't want them.'

She challenged him while her face was hidden, attending to the withered muscles in his legs.

'And what makes you think I don't? I'm only human, after all.'

He told her candidly: 'I flatter myself I know my own daughter. You haven't yet met the man who's going to light a fire in your heart. When you do, well, that'll be a different thing altogether.'

She got up, straightening her back and pushing her hair out of her eyes. 'And thank you, Aunt Jane, for your good advice. Now let's help you back in your chair. You've had enough treatment for one day.'

★ ★ ★

The following Saturday, when Miles came to pick her up in his white Citroën, Albany was all ready to leave. She was dressed in a pair of pale blue cotton sailing trousers that she had teamed with a cool white shirt and wide dark belt.

'I should bring a thick jersey,' he advised, looking at her admiringly. 'It can get very chilly in mid-channel.'

She looked surprised. 'We're not going as far as that, are we?'

He gave an amused laugh. 'I didn't mean the middle of the English Channel, half-wit. It's just a loose sailing term.'

She nodded. 'OK. I'll nip back and get one.'

Running back to the cottage she felt lighthearted. But as she went up the stairs to her room a shadow seemed to pass across the window, blocking out the sunshine. She felt herself go icy cold. At the same time the French nursery song began in her head. Goose pimples rose on her skin.

Au clair de la lune . . . mon ami Pierrot . . .

The sudden chill passed away and sunlight streamed into the room. She chided herself for being ridiculous.

Crossing the room, she opened the built-in wardrobe to take a thick blue cardigan from a hanger. The door seemed to swing open further than usual and she noticed a small gap between the top of the cupboard and the plaster that had been stuffed with a piece of paper. She took it out, surprised to find it was part of a letter. The writing was large and so untidy as to be almost indecipherable. But she could make out the last part clearly: *all my undying love, Sebastian*.

She gave an amused smile. Well, well, wouldn't Olivia Blaire have loved to find that? Suddenly Albany's mind conjured up the young man she'd seen in the photograph and she found herself wondering for a moment what it would be like to have Sebastian's undying love. And to whom had it been given?

Then she screwed the piece of paper up quickly and threw it in the wastepaper basket.

'What kept you so long?' Miles asked as Albany got into the car, tossing the cardigan onto the back seat.

'Nothing,' she told him.

'For nothing you certainly took your time.' He laughed. 'I caught a glimpse

27

of you standing by the curtain in your room looking extremely pensive. I was beginning to think you'd had second thoughts about coming sailing with me.'

He started up the engine.

'Why on earth should I do that?' she asked innocently.

He stole a quick glance at her as they set off. 'No reason. I just wondered whether anyone had been tearing my reputation to shreds, that's all.'

She widened her blue eyes intentionally. 'Don't tell me it's as bad as all that?'

'Of course not,' he grinned. 'But you know what some of these village souls are like. For years they had a local doc with one foot in the grave. Then I arrive from London and start tarting the practice up a bit, gathering a few private patients and taking on a partner. Now, for the first time in their lives they've got an efficiently-run surgery. But some people are still uncertain about a medico who happens to have red blood in his veins. Several of the village hierarchy have been trying to get me married off. But I've no intention of being caught by any of the local girls yet.'

She hid a smile. 'Why, have some of them been casting their nets your way, then?'

He gave her another quick glance. 'Perhaps. That's why I believe in safety in numbers.' He lowered his voice. 'Though all that may change when I'm ready to call it a day and settle down.'

'Oh, I see. So I'm just a make-weight, is that it?'

He gave a laugh before stopping the other side of the drive gates and getting out to close them.

A few seconds later he got back in and gave her a long look. 'You could never be a make-weight, you know that, Albany. But what I'd like to know is how an attractive girl like you hasn't been snapped up yet.'

She decided to play things extremely lightly.

'Maybe, like you, I intend making very sure before I settle down.'

He took the car along a twisting country lane that led to Hunters Cove.

'That makes sense,' he commented. 'I was very certain it wasn't for want of chances. There are only a handful of young women as pretty as you still running around loose.'

'But surely it's a woman's privilege as well as a man's to play the field?' she reproved archly.

He looked doubtful. 'Yes, well, that's as may be. But personally I'm a little old fashioned in that direction.'

'What a very chauvinistic attitude!' she exploded.

She was about to elaborate, telling him what a typically male point of view he held, when her father's words came back and she decided to let it pass.

'Maybe the real reason is that no one has lit any sort of a blaze in my heart as yet.'

Her reply pleased him. 'In that case you may find me getting out my boy scout's campfire kit one of these days and seeing what I can do.'

She laughed. 'I think you'll find me a lot harder to set fire to than you think.'

'Now I can't believe that, Albany,' he murmured. 'I really can't.'

Their afternoon together turned out to be a great success. She found his light humour and quickwittedness refreshing and stimulating. He even proved to be a good sailor and she warmed to him all the more as he taught her some of his skills, instead of expecting her to do the more mundane jobs like swilling the deck.

On the way home he told her, 'We must do this more often, Albany. You're pretty good for a girl — strong, too! Must be all that massaging!'

She laughed. 'I've enjoyed myself as well.'

He gave her a glance that spoke volumes. 'Don't you think I've been rather well behaved, not even attempting the slightest amorous advance all afternoon?'

She was still determined not to let their friendship get out of hand.

'If you had, you might have found yourself flying overboard,' she said nonchalantly. 'I once took some lessons in judo.'

'Did you now? Don't tell me you're a black belt?'

She made a swift confession. 'I didn't take them for all that long.'

He breathed a sigh. 'Phew! — that's a relief. I can't say I'm keen on macho women.' He drew the car to a halt at the Manor gates. 'Well, here we are. I'm sorry the ride back didn't take longer.'

She didn't make any comment. Instead she just smiled.

'Please don't bother to drive your car in. I'm afraid I can't ask you in for a drink. I have to get changed and go out and treat Mrs Bath-Cooper.'

He sounded genuinely dejected. 'Oh, what disappointment!' Then he looked at his watch. 'But, like you, I've other commitments as well.'

His eyes met hers. For a moment they locked. Then, before she had a chance to escape he leaned over quickly and brushed her lips with his. It was over before she realised what had happened. His bold eyes twinkled.

'There — you can't complain at that piece of leave-taking. But, my word, you do taste salty.'

She got out of the car swiftly, her cheeks slightly flushed from the unexpected embrace.

'I expect you do, too,' she said.

'Do you want to try me?' he challenged.

She shook her head, congratulating herself that his kiss had meant so little. She hadn't yet fallen under his spell.

'If you like, you can keep the offer open,' she said lightly. 'And thanks for a lovely afternoon, Miles.'

'I hope you'll agree to repeat it in the not too distant future?'

'It depends how long this spell of good weather lasts,' she said, looking up at the sky.

'Fair enough. Take care. I'll be in touch soon.'

She watched his Citroën disappear round the nearby bend before pushing open the gates and hurrying along the drive.

It was when she was half way to the cottage that she heard the sound of another car on the main road. It slowed down by the gates. She looked over her shoulder.

There was a dark coloured Porsche there. Suddenly a tall young man climbed out and opened the gates. A moment later he got back in and started driving towards her.

Albany wondered what looked so familiar about him. Then all at once she realised it was the young man in Olivia's photo, her step-son Sebastian.

He stopped as he reached the spot where she was standing. Touching a button that operated the window release he looked over at her.

'Are you going up to the Manor? Can I offer you a lift?'

His voice was deep and sent a slight thrill through her.

She shook her head. 'No, I live here.' She indicated the cottage in the drive. 'I expect you're Mr Blaire. Have you just arrived back? I hope you had a good journey home.'

He frowned, drawing together dark brows. 'Am I to understand you're living at Drive Cottage?'

She nodded.

'Who gave you permission? You're not a squatter by any chance?'

She thought it might have been a joke. But his look told her it wasn't. Suddenly she flared at him.

'No, of course I'm not. Do I look like a squatter?'

His eyes took in her windswept hair and crumpled clothes. It was then she remembered the untidy smudge of oil down the white shirt she was wearing, that she had collected from Miles' boat.

'Frankly, yes,' he said shortly.

Her cheeks flushed. 'If you *must*

know, I've been out sailing. And as to the question of who gave us permission to rent your cottage, you can ask Olivia Blaire the answer to that.'

'Olivia Blaire!'

'Yes, your step-mother. I happen to have a perfectly legal agreement that she took the trouble to have drawn up . . .'

'An agreement!' His look grew incredulous.

Albany grew more put out.

'Of course! I'd hardly be likely to rent Drive Cottage without one.'

His eyes narrowed. 'Any agreement between my step-mother and yourself is entirely null and void. Presumably you're living alone, or have you a boyfriend with you?'

The contemptuous way he said it made her even more angry.

'If it's any business of yours — which it isn't — I live with my father.'

'Oh, and does he happen to be employed in my service?'

'Hardly,' she retorted. 'He's confined

to a wheelchair. He's severely disabled.'

She saw him look further along the drive and caught sight of her father returning from the direction of the Manor.

'Is that him?' Sebastian asked.

She nodded.

He remained silent before relenting.

'Very well — you can stay on at the cottage until I've thrashed this thing out. But I can assure you that any agreement you have is entirely illegal. Olivia has never asked my permission.'

Before she could think of anything to reply, he had slipped his magnificent car into gear and driven away, leaving her to glare after him.

Darrel Edmunds wheeled himself up to her.

'I've just been borrowing a few books from the Manor library. Who was that? Olivia didn't say she was expecting a visitor.'

Albany's temper died down. There was certainly no point in alarming her father unnecessarily.

'That,' she said, giving him an affectionate kiss on his brow, 'happens to be Olivia's long-lost step-son, just returned from his travels.'

'You don't say! I expect he and his step-mother will have plenty to talk about.'

'I wouldn't be surprised,' she said enigmatically.

Later that evening her father tackled her when she came home from treating Mrs Bath-Cooper.

'I've been sitting here doing some worrying,' he told her.

'Why?' she asked, taking her coat off and hanging it in the closet.

'I'm not at all happy about that agreement we have with Olivia Blaire. You've promised me several times you'd let me see it, but each time you've conveniently forgotten.'

'Silly! It's just an ordinary agreement.'

'I'm not so sure till I've seen it. I'm afraid that if Mr Blaire objects to us being here, the only decent thing will be for us to leave. It's not as though we couldn't find somewhere else.'

'That's not as easy as you think,' she said, digging her heels in. 'There are no other cottages in Petersville. And I've only just started to build up a nice little clientèle of some of Miles Planter's patients.'

Darrel heaved a sigh. 'It's just that I happened to catch sight of your expression as Mr Blaire drove away. While you were out I put two and two together and guessed you'd had words, probably over that agreement.'

She shook her head defiantly. 'As far as I'm concerned that agreement is perfectly valid. And even if it wasn't he could hardly put us out on the streets after the large deposit I paid.'

He frowned. 'You've never mentioned anything about a deposit. You'd better let me see that agreement at once.'

Albany went upstairs to fetch it without switching on the light. At the top of the stairs she came to an abrupt halt as a feeling of iciness swept over her once again.

3

By the time Sebastian reached the Manor his stepmother had already heard the car and was waiting near the sitting-room window. Her eyebrows rose when she saw who her visitor was. Her dead husband's son! And he hadn't even bothered to write and let her know he was returning.

The corners of her mouth turned down. Maybe it was his intention to surprise her? He had every right. He happened to own the place. She was merely an uninvited guest: someone who had begged entrance.

For the truth was that Sebastian had never suggested she sold Lakeview as she had told Albany and her father. It had been forced on her by her creditors. She had been overspending as usual and had had to ring Sebastian as a last resort.

He had been reluctant at first to let her move into Blaire Manor. But she had pleaded, pretending to weep over the phone in order to force his hand. And he had given in as she had hoped he would.

Very few people knew it, but she and her step-son had never hit it off. She had been years younger than his father, and Sebastian had suspected at the very beginning that she had only married for money.

She gave a petulant shrug. So what if that had been the case? She had given Timothy Blaire a lot in return. Loyalty and fidelity. And for most of their marriage they had been fairly happy. She hadn't been underhand. Timothy had known from the beginning that she didn't love him. But they had been compatible — at least, most of the time.

Any quarrels they had ever had had been over money. She had been under the impression that Timothy would inherit everything on the death of his rich and unmarried brother. But that had not been the case. For once Timothy had outwitted her, persuading his brother to leave everything to Sebastian instead. She hadn't found out until after the funeral.

Her thin, over-made-up lips tightened. Was that any reason to grow fonder of Sebastian? If it had been left to Timothy *she* would have inherited the lot. As it was, it had taken an extremely short time to run through what she had.

Sebastian's footsteps grew louder as he strode along the hall and Olivia steeled herself for their meeting. She felt her heart pounding. With luck he would not yet have learned that she had let Drive Cottage. Though it was possible he had met Darrel Edmunds on his way home.

The door opened, and the coldly accusing gaze Sebastian gave her told her that he already knew. There was nothing for it now but to try to brazen things out.

She put on her most welcoming smile. 'Why, my dear boy, what a lovely surprise. I never expected you back so soon. I was under the impression you were still in North Africa, or South Africa, or the Equator, or, or, somewhere . . .'

Sebastian threw her welcome aside. 'Let's not fool ourselves, Olivia. My return may be a surprise but it's certainly not agreeable to you, so you can stop pretending.'

Her smile faded. She put on a pained expression instead.

'Oh, Sebastian — I thought that was all over. I thought you'd begun to like me a little . . .'

'Like you! After you'd done your level best to poison everyone's minds against me? Fortunately, in the case of my father and uncle, you didn't succeed. But let's get things clear. I told you you could stay at Blaire Manor for a short, interim period while you sorted out your affairs. You've been here over six months, long enough to get on your feet and make alternative arrangements. I hope that's the case because I want you out of here within a week!'

'Oh, Sebastian: how can you be so cruel and insensitive?'

'Easily! After the misery you've put me through in the past. But we'll forget that for the moment. I've something more important to discuss.' His eyes blazed. 'I understand you've had the audacity to let part of my property in my absence?'

She saw there was no use in denying it and gave a sigh of resignation.

'I suppose you mean Drive Cottage?'

'Of course I mean Drive Cottage! Or have you let part of the Manor as well?'

'Oh don't be so ridiculous, Sebastian!'

He waited for an explanation. She shrugged and tried to make light of the situation.

'I really don't know what all the fuss is about. The cottage was already furnished, if a bit dusty and untidy.

And it seemed such a pity to let it stand idle with so many people crying out for accommodation.'

'You had no right, no right at all!'

She realised he was losing his temper and was quick to take advantage.

'Really, Sebastian, you should learn to take a grip of yourself. Anyone would think I'd committed some heinous crime.'

'But you *have*! You've let Drive Cottage without permission. How dare you! How *dare* you!'

She drew herself up self-righteously. 'I dared because it seemed the only right and proper thing to do. The girl happens to be an old school friend of my nephew Robert's wife. She was sorely in need of a quiet place where her father could convalesce. He happens to have been paralysed in a bomb outrage, and his daughter's a qualified physiotherapist!'

Sebastian listened to her before replying with scorn.

'Knowing you as I do, I hardly

think you were moved so much by compassion as by the thought of monetary gain. Just how much have you let it for? And you'd better come up with the truth.'

She told him reluctantly, hedging over the large deposit she'd insisted on.

'And I presume it's gone straight into your pocket,' he accused.

She had the grace to redden. 'Naturally, Sebastian, I intended to pay you back every penny.'

He gave her a look which showed how much he despised her.

'Never mind! Just start packing and be out of Blaire Manor within seven days, or I shall put the whole business in the hands of solicitors!'

As he disappeared abruptly from the room, Olivia allowed herself a small smile. Sebastian would never do that, she felt sure. He would be far too afraid of the publicity. All the same, it was fortunate she had managed to save part of the money. It would be something to fall back on if he made it too uncomfortable for her to stay.

In the meantime Sebastian had taken the stairs up to his room two at a time. Striding into his bedroom he went over to the window and stared out. The chimneys of Drive Cottage were just visible between the trees.

He could barely take in what he had learned. Olivia had had the audacity to let Drive Cottage, the place where Corinne had lived. He had left it just the way it had been the day — the day he had followed her to Hunters Cove. The day she had disappeared forever from his life. And now someone else was there.

If he had hoped to drive her memory from his mind by staying away for a year he had hoped in vain. Recollection of that last day was still as clear in his mind as ever. He supposed it always would be.

And now, on top of that, he had to decide whether to honour Olivia's agreement with the new tenants. He lay down on the bed and put his hands under his head, reliving the past with all its bitter-sweetness.

★ ★ ★

For the next few days Albany was kept busy with a batch of new patients. On several occasions she spied Sebastian from a distance, but he made no attempt to call at the cottage and discuss the agreement.

When she had shown it to her father, he had told her bluntly that it wasn't even worth the paper it was written on. Olivia had used a firm of solicitors from a town some distance away who had not realised she wasn't the true owner. Without Sebastian's signature, or written permission, the agreement was null and void.

She reminded him about the large deposit she had paid and Darrel had agreed reluctantly to wait until Sebastian tackled them before taking any action. In the meantime they both stayed away from the Manor.

It was more than a week after Sebastian's return that she met the blazing headlights of his Porsche as she was driving through the gates late one evening. There was no room for them both to pass so she stopped and reversed into the main road to let him by.

He thanked her by flashing his lights on and off. Then he drew to a halt by her side window.

'You should have let me back up!'

'I'm sorry,' she said shortly. 'I *will* next time.'

He studied her for a moment. 'About that agreement you have with my stepmother.'

Albany grew apprehensive. 'Yes!'

He gave a small smile. 'It's entirely invalid, but under the circumstances I've decided to honour it. If you let me have it some time I'll add my signature to it.'

She had not really known what to

expect and his words came as an immense relief.

She let out an impromptu sigh. 'That's very kind of you, Mr Blaire.'

He took in her relieved expression by the light of their dipped headlights.

'Not at all. It seems you rented the cottage in good faith and paid a very large deposit. I don't see why you and your father should be the ones to suffer since you're innocent parties.'

His manner was so different to that displayed at their first meeting that she could only sit and stare and repeat her thanks.

He wished her goodnight and drove off in the direction of Petersville. She drove on to the cottage, leaving the gates open for his return.

When she told her father about their meeting and the words they had exchanged he looked pleased.

'I must say it's a comfort to have that ironed out. I expect Olivia's managed to talk him round. I'm not keen on her but she's a very persuasive woman. According to her, that step-son of hers is a very spoilt young man, the apple of his father's eye. Apparently, he tried to drive a wedge between husband and wife the moment they were married: sponged on them and didn't bother to pay it back after he came into his uncle's fortune. It's the reason she was left so hard-up after her husband's death, she tells me.' He gave Albany a sage look. 'But how much of that is a jealous woman's imagination, and how much is truth, we'll never know. Anyway, I'm glad you've met and sorted things out. I've grown quite attached to this cottage. It's very tranquil.'

'That's derived from a French word, isn't it?'

He nodded. 'I believe so.'

She grew thoughtful. 'I wonder why you used it instead of peaceful.'

He laughed. 'Is it all that important?'

She kissed his cheek. 'Not at all. I just feel this cottage has very French connections. You can blame it on my intuition.'

He reached up and took her hand.

'You can go to bed and dream tranquil dreams now,' she said. 'I'll bring you a cuppa and settle you down in half an hour.'

He gave her hand a squeeze before releasing it.

'Thanks, love, many thanks.'

She looked after him fondly as he wheeled himself over to his bedroom. Then she ran lightly up the stairs, taking off her coat as she went. At the top she stopped abruptly as she'd grown into the habit of doing. But there was no feeling of sudden chill tonight. Maybe the ghost was laid.

She knew if she wasn't careful she'd have herself believing in the supernatural. And that would never do, coming from someone in a practical profession such as herself. But there had been several times in her life when she had felt odd kinds of vibrations. She had felt them intensely the day her mother had died. Maybe she was psychic!

She switched on the light and went over to draw the curtains. As she did so she caught sight of Sebastian's Porsche returning. He hadn't been out for long. Maybe he had only popped out to post a letter in the village.

As she got undressed she found herself going over their short meeting, wondering what had happened to make him so affable. Maybe, as her father had suggested, Olivia had got round him. All the same, it had been an extremely foolish thing for her to do, to rent them the cottage without his knowledge. No wonder he had been so furious.

She wondered whether there was any truth in Olivia's story of him sponging. He certainly didn't look the type. There was nothing mean-eyed about him. In fact, the more she thought about him, the nicer he looked. His dark eyes actually had a warm, friendly look. And his mouth was generous.

His lips weren't full, but they were a very pleasant shape. And his chin was determined, with the smallest of clefts in the centre.

She blushed, surprising herself at how much she had taken in about him. She caught sight of her heightened colour as she glanced in the dressing table mirror and tried to put him out of her mind.

Sebastian Blaire was really no concern of hers. He was an extemely rich, very good looking and probably horribly spoilt young man. She doubted if he even had a care in the world, except where his next half million was coming from!

Then, for no reason, she remembered the letter he had written, signed *all my undying love, Sebastian*, and wondered to whom it had been written.

Who had rented the cottage before them? Maybe it would be interesting to find out.

And then, as though in answer to her question, a photograph fell out onto the carpet as she opened a drawer to get out a fresh nightie. She looked at it in astonishment and bent to pick it up.

A dark haired young woman smiled back at her; her high cheekbones accentuated a pair of extraordinarily fine eyes. There was something knowledgeable and challenging in their expression. The young woman certainly didn't seem to lack confidence. Albany thought she had a continental look about her. She saw there was a signature scrawled across the bottom. Corinne!

She wondered where the photograph had dropped from, and felt beneath the drawer. It was coarse and uneven. If the drawer had been over-full at any stage a photo might easily have been able to lodge there.

After studying it again for several minutes, she put it back in the drawer amongst her underclothes for safe keeping.

★ ★ ★

A few days later, Albany met Miles Planter in the Petersville Arms for a lunchtime beer. It was a well-known haunt for a lot of the young professionals. But she considered it to be a little pseudo with too many pieces of highly polished brass, and too much red velvet plush. However, it was one of Miles' favourite places. He always looked very much at home there amongst other members of the yachting fraternity.

Once they'd exhausted several other topics of conversation she managed to bring the talk round skilfully to Sebastian Blaire's unexpected return.

'How well do you know each other?' she asked.

'Not well.'

'He's not one of your patients, then?'

He shook his head.

'Were you here before he took over the Manor or did you come after?'

'We came about the same time.'

'Do you know what he does for his living?'

Miles gave a smile. 'Why the questionnaire?'

She grew flustered. 'Sorry, I was just slightly interested since he happens to be my landlord.' She paused. 'By the way, did you ever meet a person called Corinne, who probably had the cottage before us?'

Her question badly startled him. For a moment he lost his lazy smile. Then it came back again.

'Who's been talking to you about Corinne — surely not Blaire himself?'

She told him the truth. 'I found a photograph. It dropped out of a drawer in my room. The girl in it signed herself Corinne. I thought it was likely she'd lived at Drive Cottage before us, or at least stayed there at some time.'

He studied a row of shiny horse brasses and sipped his drink before replying. Then he gave a resigned sigh.

'You're right in thinking she lived at the cottage before you. But it was a long time ago, easily a year. Blaire left the Manor not long after she disappeared, presumed drowned. I thought, after the torrid affair they'd had, he was leaving the cottage just as she'd left it, as a memorial to her. That's why I was mildly surprised when you turned up at the surgery and told me you were living there.'

Albany stared at him. 'Drowned, did you say?'

He nodded. 'Her clothes were found on the beach at Hunters Cove, about a mile across the fields from the cottage. She often used to go there. It's not the safest of beaches. There's a vicious undertow. But she was a strong swimmer. I took her out in the boat a few times.'

'You knew her well?'

'Fairly well. But not as well as Sebastian Blaire, naturally.'

'Were they engaged?'

He drained his glass before replying. 'I've no idea. You'd better ask him. I really must be getting back. I've an ante-natal clinic at two.'

By his manner she knew she'd upset him.

'What have I said?' she asked.

He looked down at her, studying the flecks of gold that danced in her eyes.

'My dear Albany, if you don't know you must be extraordinarily insensitive.'

Her gaze saddened. 'I'm very sorry, Miles. I didn't realise you were in love with her. My questions must have wounded you.'

He gave a laugh. 'You've got the wrong end of the stick, Albany. I liked Corinne, but I certainly wasn't in love with her.'

'Then why — I don't understand!'

'Don't you?' he said, raising an eyebrow. 'You spend all the lunch hour asking questions about another man, and then expect me to be not in the slightest degree jealous. Shame on you, Albany!'

She felt her colour rise. Had she really spent the whole time asking about Sebastian or had he made it up?

'I'm glad to see you looking suitably ashamed,' he commented. Then he consulted his watch. 'I *must* go. How about coming sailing with me next weekened?'

She felt she owed it to him. 'Fine!'

'Right, I'll call for you about two on Saturday.'

He gave her arm a little squeeze before parting from her on the cobbled pavement outside the popular pub.

For the rest of that afternoon Albany's mind was taken up with what she had learned. The new patient she went to treat willingly added more.

Mrs Petty was a wealthy widow who lived in a large house on the edge of the village. Her leg had recently come out of plaster. Albany showed her how to exercise it. The woman used the time as an excuse to gossip.

'Dear Doctor Planter mentioned that you'd come to live at Drive Cottage. That's on the Blaire estate, isn't it? The cottage where the girl who drowned used to live?'

'You mean Corinne?'

'I see you know her name. You probably know all about the tragedy as well?'

'No, only a little.'

The woman was only too pleased to talk about it.

'She came to the district a short while before Mr Blaire. She'd rented the cottage from Major Royal who owned the Manor at the time. So when Sebastian Blaire bought the estate she was what is known as a sitting tenant. He couldn't have got her out, even if he'd wanted, which, of course he didn't, because it was well known he was smitten with her. She was a very beautiful girl — dark and rather Latin looking. With an extremely attractive accent, because, naturally with a name like Corinne Latour, she was French . . . '

Albany gave a small gasp. 'Did you say French?'

'Yes, I did. What's the matter? You've gone quite pale.'

Albany recovered herself quickly. 'It's really nothing. Please go on with what you were saying.'

'Now where was I? Ah, yes! He wasn't alone in thinking she was rather special, because a lot of the young men in the district thought the same. Doctor Planter in particular, I believe, since they often went sailing together. And it was such a tragedy when her clothes were found at Hunters Cove that day. Because, as everyone knew, she was a very good swimmer. It was assumed by a lot of people that she'd committed suicide. But why would such a beautiful girl like that want to commit suicide?' Mrs Petty shook her head and answered her own question. 'No, it was much more likely she got caught in the strong offshore wind and was taken out to sea.'

'So her body was never found?'

'No, but that's not so unusual in these parts. There's many a fisherman who's been washed overboard in a gale and his body never seen again.'

'It must have been a terrible shock for Sebastian?'

'Oh, my dear, I've never seen a more broken man. For days he looked as though a square meal had never passed his lips. It was quite soon afterwards that he went away. I heard he gave instructions that the cottage was not to be touched. But how true that is, I wouldn't like to say, since you're living there now and Sebastian's home again. Maybe he's managed to get over it, poor man — '

Albany interrupted her in full flow.

'There, Mrs Petty, if you just keep up those exercises I've shown you, your leg muscles will get stronger.'

She gathered up her things. Reluctantly the older woman had her shown out.

Albany drove home thoughtfully, turning over in her mind all that she'd been told. She found it quite understandable that Sebastian had been furious the first time they'd met. It seemed Olivia had callously had all trace of the dead girl swept away. Although, since she'd only lived at the Manor for six months, she probably hadn't known about their love affair.

So Corinne had been French. Albany wasn't really surprised. It was true, she must be psychic. Maybe she was in the wrong profession!

But the most intriguing thing of all was, why couldn't she seem to get the thought of Sebastian Blaire out of her mind? And why could she hardly wait to set eyes on him again?

4

The third Thursday in August had been arranged in advance for Darrel's periodical check-up at Bridesmay Hospital near Oxford. Albany had been careful to keep it free.

As they drove the hundred miles there in the Fiesta they chatted easily. She recalled his withdrawn behaviour of less than two months ago, and marvelled at how well he seemed to be progressing. The staff of the hospital would notice a big difference.

She was certain now, that although it had been a wrench, leaving the district where they'd lived had been a wise move. If she'd kept on her job at the clinic attached to the hospital, and they'd lived together in the house he'd shared with her mother, it would have taken infinitely longer to get over her death. As it was, she often felt the loss almost as much as her father. It was still too soon to talk about that bright-eyed, girlish-figured, lovely lady, without feeling close to tears.

At the hospital the receptionist remembered them both well and cast an eye over Darrel's papers.

'So you'll be spending a couple of nights with us, Mr Edmunds,' she said, looking up and smiling.

Albany was surprised. 'I'm sorry, nothing about staying was mentioned on the appointment card. I didn't realise it was normal procedure. I'm afraid I haven't packed any pyjamas or washing tackle for him.'

'That's all right. I'm sure we can find some things for him. If you'd like to pop out and buy him the basic essentials, like a toothbrush and razor, I'll have him admitted and up in the ward by the time you get back.'

Albany glanced down at her father who was frowning in an uncertain way.

'Are you sure you'll be all right on

your own for a couple of nights?' he asked.

She smiled reassuringly. 'Of course. I shall take the opportunity of moving the furniture around in your room. You've been complaining about the moonlight shining in on your face and keeping you awake.'

'That's all very well, but I don't like the idea of you shifting heavy furniture around on your own without me being there to supervise.'

'Stop worrying. If it will please you, I'll ask Rose who works at the Manor to give me a hand.'

'I'm sure it can't be necessary for me to spend two nights here.'

'No arguments,' she said shaking her head. 'We're holding people up. Here comes a porter to take you up to your ward. I'll buy those things and be back in ten minutes.'

She dashed off before he could protest further. At a nearby chemist she bought all he needed. When she went back, one of the specialists was already with him. Rather than unsettle him again she left the things with the ward sister.

'Give him my love, won't you? And tell him I'll pick him up again about ten on Saturday morning.'

The sister promised.

Taking her time, Albany went back to the car feeling slightly lost. It seemed like returning in time to be leaving her father in Bridesmay Hospital again. And she wasn't too sure she liked the idea of spending two nights on her own at Drive Cottage. She was pleased now that she hadn't mentioned anything to him about the strange sensations she'd sometimes felt there.

She took the three-hour run home at an easy pace, and instead of going directly back, she took the car down to Hunters Cove and treated herself to a ploughman's lunch in the small friendly pub. It was vastly different to the opulence of the Petersville Arms, and was used by fishermen and locals instead of 'yachties'.

It was while she was there she remembered she'd promised to go sailing with Miles the following Saturday. She could hardly do that if she had to fetch her father. Even though they would probably be home before two, she wouldn't feel like leaving him on his own the minute they were back.

Bearing it in mind to get in touch with him later, she finished her lunch and took a stroll round the tiny harbour, inspecting the boats, and catching sight of Miles' streamlined craft in its usual mooring. Continuing to the end of the jetty, she stood there to admire the view for a while before turning back. It was then she received a pleasant surprise. Coming towards her, dressed more casually than she'd seen him before, in a pair of worn jeans and a tee shirt, was Sebastian Blaire.

She noticed his bare arms were richly sun-tanned. His body seemed to have the lithe grace of a panther. She was astonished at the uprated beating of her heart. At the same time he noticed her and gave a pleased smile.

'Hello,' she said, trying not to sound breathless. 'Fancy meeting you. Do you happen to have a boat here as well?'

He looked mystified. 'As well as *you*, do you mean?'

She laughed. 'No, I meant as well as Miles — er — Doctor Planter, that is.'

He seemed to savour the information before replying.

'No, I'm not really the sailing type.'

She looked back into his eyes, which now that she saw him close to, she could see were dark grey, and felt an overwhelming desire to know him better. What kind of type *was* he? Had he had a career before he was left his uncle's money? Why had he bought a place like Blaire Manor if he was rarely in England? How long would he decide to stay this time?

'You're not working this afternoon, then?' he commented.

'No — I've just driven back from Oxfordshire. I've left my father in hospital for a few days.'

'Nothing serious?' he asked quickly.

She shook her head. 'No, just a check-up.'

They began to walk back towards the harbour chatting.

'Is there any hope of him recovering the use of his legs?' Sebastian asked.

'None whatsoever,' she said sadly.

'Would you like to tell me how it happened?'

She put him in the picture, marvelling once more at how sympathetic he seemed to have become since their first, unfortunate, meeting. At that time she'd been prepared to think him a spoilt, pugnacious snob. And now all that had changed.

She looked up into his warm intelligent gaze. Oh, why did her heart play such tricks when she was with him?

When they reached the spot where she'd parked her Fiesta, she spied his Porsche parked close by. For a foolish second she wondered whether he'd recognised it and parked there on purpose before coming in search of her. But she pushed the thought away quickly. Sebastian Blaire couldn't have the slightest interest in following her.

Without really wanting to leave him she began to unlock the door of her car.

'Are you going back to the cottage?' he asked.

She nodded. 'I suppose so. But it will seem strange going back to an empty place. It's the reason I had lunch here. I'm used to father being about, if only wheeling himself around your grounds.'

He made a swift suggestion. 'Since we're both at a loose end, why don't we join forces? I was thinking of driving into Abbotsbury to choose some pottery. How does that appeal to you?'

She felt her pleasure increase. 'It sounds better than the treat *I'd* planned: moving father's bedroom furniture around.'

He looked slightly bewildered.

She gave a laugh. 'It's just that he's been complaining that the moon shines in on his face when he's asleep,' she explained.

'Oh, I see,' he smiled.

She re-locked her car and they took his. It was exhilarating to be sitting beside Sebastian as he drove smoothly along the country lanes. She examined his strong profile from beneath her eye lashes without making it obvious.

His dark tan accentuated his good looks. She imagined him lying idly on a warm, African beach to acquire it.

'Have you always lived around here?' she asked.

'No, most of my childhood was spent in the Lake District. How about you?'

'Oh, I've always lived near Oxford, even when I was at college.'

'And how do you like being a physio?'

'Very much. But, to be honest,' she confessed, 'I enjoyed treating the people who came to my last clinic more than the ones I treat here.'

'Why's that?'

'I suppose I felt more sorry for them. Most of the people I treat now are extremely wealthy. The ones I treated before were a mixed bag, mainly National Health patients.' She paused. 'Maybe that makes me an inverted snob.'

He raised an eyebrow. 'Sometimes people can't help being wealthy, you know. Often it's an added responsibility.'

'I've never heard a rich person complaining.'

'You sound prejudiced. If you did I expect you'd think they were lying.'

'What did you do before you bought Blaire Manor?' she asked curiously.

He seemed to find her question amusing. 'The same as I do now.'

She was surprised. 'You mean you've never had a job?'

In answer he gave a laugh.

'What's so funny?' she asked disappointedly. 'I find it difficult to believe that anyone can lead such a totally selfish life. If I was in your place I'd become extremely bored.'

He took his eyes off the road for just long enough to give her an interested glance.

'Perhaps you would. But we can't all be the same, you know, Albany.'

She went quiet, wishing she hadn't asked such a pertinent question since the answer was not to her liking. In her heart of hearts she had hoped he was more than he appeared to be, that he'd spent the last year following a worthwhile pursuit instead of swanning uselessly around the world, probably staying at the best hotels and seeing sights far beyond the reach of most people's bank accounts.

The drive to Abbotsbury took less time than she had anticipated. Sebastian parked his car in the main street and they got out and walked to the nearest potter's.

She tried to forget her disappointment in him, staring into the window while they admired some of the pieces. It wasn't difficult to find herself warming to him again.

He pointed to a large blue vase. 'Don't you think that would look nice filled with grasses? There used to be one in the cottage once, but I notice my step-mother has had it brought up to the house.'

Albany remembered that she had seen one on the corner cupboard in Drive Cottage the first time she had looked over it.

'Oh, I couldn't possibly accept something so expensive,' she began.

He reminded her: 'You're forgetting that the cottage is let to you furnished. I believe I'm entitled to replace the vase.'

Her embarrassment increased. How ridiculous to assume he was buying it for her! She tried to cover her confusion.

'Very well, but if you put expensive pieces into the cottage you do so at your peril. Father's inclined to knock against the furniture with his wheelchair sometimes. And I can be very butterfingered when I'm doing the housework.'

He looked down at her in surprise. 'You mean you do your own housework as well as going out to treat patients?'

'Of course.'

He put his foot down. 'Well, that I'm not going to allow. You've paid an extremely large deposit and I naturally assumed that included the use of Rose two or three times a week.'

She accepted his offer gratefully. 'If you really mean that it'll be a great help. I've been getting much busier with clients lately. I'd seriously considered getting someone in, but most of the women in the village are accounted for.'

'Then think no more of it. Rose shall clean for you three times a week at my expense. That still leaves plenty of help up at the house.' He slipped his arm into hers companionably. 'Now, you've no more excuses about me buying the blue pot for you, have you?'

She felt a warm glow run through her at his touch. She had never experienced anything quite like it before. It was like fire that coursed through her veins, thrilling her to the core.

The potter, a middle-aged man in a green overall, came into the shop from a workroom next door as soon as they entered. It was obvious that he remembered Sebastian from some time past. His face lit up.

'Long time, no see, sir.' He stretched out a slender hand for Sebastian to shake. 'Been away then? To warmer climes by the look of it. We don't often get a chance to turn that colour in this country.'

Sebastian replied measuredly. 'Yes, I've been away.'

'Might one enquire where?'

'Africa, mostly.'

The potter shook his head affably. 'Bit too warm for me there. I'll stick to the UK, in spite of its awful winters.' He grew thoughtful, putting up a long finger to stroke his cheek. 'If I'm not mistaken you bought a large blue vase the very first time you came in here. You said it would look nice with coloured grasses in for the young lady's cottage.' He took a closer look at Albany. 'But I'm wrong, it wasn't this young lady, was it, sir? No, if I recall, it was a darkhaired, foreign looking girl . . .'

Sebastian glared and the man caught his look and reddened. He began to stammer uncomfortably.

'Dearie me, I hope I haven't gone and put my big foot in it. My wife is always telling me I talk too much. This time I'm inclined to agree with her. Well, well, what can I do for you? Or are you just looking around?'

Albany sensed Sebastian's annoyance. He seemed to have grown paler in spite of his sun tan. What a fool the potter was to remind him of Corinne Latour. It was evidently the French girl for whom he'd bought the blue pot that Olivia had taken a fancy to. And now their afternoon was spoilt.

Sebastian steered her out of the shop. 'Perhaps we'll return some other time.'

They left the potter's and walked back to the car without talking. Albany left him alone with his memories, feeling like an interloper. Clouds gathered across a day that had seemed perfect. Now it looked like rain.

As they drove back towards Petersville she glanced several times at his set expression, wishing she could share his sadness. But he'd grown miles away from her.

'Sorry about that,' he said with a thoughtful smile when they were nearly at Hunters Cove.

'It doesn't matter,' she replied, pretending she thought he was talking about the vase. 'You're entitled to change your mind about buying it. I'm merely your tenant.'

He frowned. 'Don't say it like that. I don't feel like your landlord. I'd sooner be your friend.'

'There's no reason why you shouldn't

be both,' she said lightly.

'Let me take you out for tea, then.'

She shook her head. 'I'm not really hungry. I had a large lunch.'

He stopped his car near hers. 'What will you do now? Ah, yes — go home and shift the furniture around.'

She smiled. 'That's right. Thanks for the drive, Sebastian. I enjoyed it.'

His eyes looked into hers with disbelief. 'Don't tell fibs. I ruined it for you, promising to buy you something and not doing it.'

'Don't be silly. I didn't think of it for me. It was for your cottage.'

'All right, for the cottage, then. Don't let's split hairs. But, in that case, you can leave that corner place free. I'll get something else.' He leaned over quickly and kissed her cheek. 'See you later!'

She looked back at him in a startled way before getting out. Then she watched him drive off before unlocking the door of her Fiesta.

5

After Sebastian had driven out of sight, Albany got into her car and went back to Drive Cottage. Her mind was full of Sebastian's unexpected kiss.

Why had he done such an impulsive thing? They hardly knew each other. They had only been out for a short country drive together, and part of that had been undertaken in silence.

Her pulse raced at the memory of what his closeness had done to her. She was beside herself with a kind of ecstasy for most of the drive home.

Then, searching in her pocket for the key to unlock the cottage, she suddenly remembered Miles Planter. She had not yet rung him to let him know she wouldn't be able to go sailing with him on Saturday. She gave a glance at her watch. Hopefully he would not have started surgery.

'What a nice surprise!' he said after the receptionist had put Albany through. 'How are you? I missed seeing you in the Arms this lunchtime. Have you been very busy?'

'I thought you'd remember I had to take father to Bridesmay Hospital.'

'Ah, yes — how did you get on?'

'I shan't see his specialist till Saturday. That's why I'm having to ring you. Unfortunately, I won't be able to come sailing. They're keeping father in for two days. I'm fetching him home Saturday morning. I doubt if we'll get home before three.'

He took a moment or two to answer. Then he sounded genuinely disappointed as though she had spoiled a special treat. 'Ah, that's a pity. I've been really looking forward to it.'

'I'm sorry,' she said, without particularly feeling it. 'Perhaps some other time.'

'OK. Well, some other time it is.'

A wall of silence seemed to descend. Albany frantically tried to think of something else to say instead of just hanging up. Then Miles went on unexpectedly.

'By the way, did you enjoy your afternoon out with Sebastian Blaire?'

She gave a little gasp. He heard it and gave a short laugh.

'I bet that surprised you, didn't it? You didn't think you'd be found out so soon.' He chided her with a touch of hardness in his tone. 'It's clear I was right to feel aggrieved the other day. You're obviously starry-eyed about the man. But be warned, Albany! Sebastian was over the moon about Corinne Latour. When a man loves a woman *that* much he never gets her out of his system.'

'How ridiculous you're being!' she burst out angrily. 'It was purely by chance I met Sebastian this afternoon. And for your information I hardly know him, so it's impossible to be *starry-eyed* about him, as you term it.'

'Really! My source of information

swears they saw you in a clinch in his car.'

'That's a lie! Who's spreading the rumours?'

'My new receptionist, actually. She's quite a girl, slim, dark and leggy. But a bit on the gossipy side. She told me a moment ago when she came in that she'd seen you both at Hunters Cove.'

There was another long silence while Albany considered. It was clear the girl had seen Sebastian's brief peck and magnified it out of all proportion. But why did she have to explain that to Miles?

'I think, if I was you,' she said coolly, 'I'd beware of passing on information like that. It might some day rebound on you.'

He laughed. 'Too late. They've already had a field day with me. They're on the lookout for a fresh victim.' He grew serious again. 'But watch out, Albany. Men like Blaire don't stay in one place very long. I wouldn't like to be the one to have to perform heart surgery on you when he does another twelve-month flit from the Manor.'

She put down the receiver, pretending they'd been accidentally cut off, and looked down at it angrily. How dare he give her his advice? He was merely piqued because she'd turned down his invitation to go sailing. She compared the two men in her mind. Miles Planter came out badly. Although he was a clever doctor he was also a playboy and a womaniser. Sebastian might be idle, but he had all the appearance of an honest, sincere person.

Nevertheless, she hoped their disagreement didn't put Miles off sending her other referrals. She had started to build up a worthwhile practice. It would be a shame if her hard work was jeopardised.

She tried to put the incident out of her mind by rearranging the furniture in her father's room.

The bed and dressing table of carved

oak were both a lot heavier than they looked. She had to give up completely where the matching wardrobe was concerned. But an hour later she stood back glowing to admire her handiwork, and was satisfied that there was now no chance of the moon being able to cast its light directly onto his bed.

The more she thought about it, the more it seemed a fair possibility that it hadn't been the moon, anyway. It was much more likely to be the same phenomena she'd experienced in her own room just above. Will-o-the-wisp lights often came and went as she was trying to get off to sleep. She had put it down to the lights of traffic on the nearby road rather than give it any supernatural connotation.

When her strenuous efforts were completed she decided to have a shower, and chose her father's bathroom since it was nearer. Half way through she caught the sound of the doorbell and breathed an impatient sigh. Who could it be? If she didn't answer, maybe they'd go away. No, it might be something important.

She switched off the shower and wrapped herself in her father's royal blue, shortie, towelling robe. Dripping wet she padded out of his room and across the sitting room carpet.

'Hold on, I'm coming as fast as I can!' she called as the doorbell rang again.

Leaving damp footprints on the polished parquet flooring of the hall, she stopped to try to make out the shape of the caller through the partially glassed front door. It looked like a tall stout man. A warning voice told her it would be extremely unwise to open the door without some form of reassurance as to his identity.

'Who is it?' she asked uncertainly.

'Sebastian!' came the answer.

'Goodness, it doesn't look like you!' But she'd have known his voice anywhere from the way it quickened her pulse rate.

'What's up?' he asked through the

door. 'I haven't come at a bad time, have I? You weren't in the bath, by any chance?'

She gave a laugh. 'No, the shower, as a matter of fact.'

'Lord, I'm sorry. Look, I'll come back when it's more convenient.'

'No, don't do that,' she said quickly. The thought of him leaving without knowing why he'd called was too much.

Her fingers trembled as she lifted the catch. When the door was open she saw he was carrying a huge parcel. It was the reason he'd looked fat.

'Goodness, what's in there?'

Sebastian studied her brief apparel with interest. She could feel his gaze sweep down and stop at the hem of her father's shortie dressing gown. She clutched it round her more tightly.

'You'd better come in,' she said.

He followed her, apologising. 'There's nothing worse than having to interrupt a shower to answer some nitwit at the door.'

His look seemed to have melted her limbs. She could feel her heart doing a jig against her ribs.

'Pour yourself a drink and make yourself at home while I get dressed,' she said, making for the stairs. Over her shoulder she called, 'There's Scotch or gin in the corner cupboard. You'll find tonic or what-you-will in the fridge.'

'Can I pour you something as well?' he called after her.

She considered the shock he had given her.

'A small brandy mightn't come amiss! It's in the same place as the gin.'

She studied her reflection in the long bedroom mirror as she hurriedly put on a pair of blue jeans and a plaid shirt. Her cheeks looked bright and her eyes sparkled with excitement.

She looked away, ashamed at the way she was behaving. Anyone would think she was a teenager instead of a woman of twenty-eight.

Her father's words came back to her.

Was it possible she had found the man capable of setting her heart on fire? Thoughtfully she ran a comb through her long hair, tying it into a pony tail like a young girl before hurrying downstairs.

Sebastian gave her an admiring look as he handed her her drink.

'How quick you've been.'

She took a sip of the brandy to calm her nerves.

'Why have you come?' she asked, deliberately keeping her tone light. Then she remembered his parcel and looked around. 'What have you done with your huge package?'

She saw it almost at once and gave a gasp. It was a large, cut-glass vase that must have cost him the earth. He had placed it in the empty spot she'd left over the corner cupboard.

'I think it would look nice filled with red roses,' he said quietly. 'I'll get Jefferson to pick you some tomorrow.'

'You mustn't do that. I told you I was butterfingered. What on earth would you say if I told you I'd dropped it?'

He studied her. 'Accidents happen. In that case I'd have to buy you another.'

'Oh, look, I can't possibly accept it.'

'Of course you will, because I want you to.'

Her longing for him grew. But she shook it away out of jealousy over the dead girl. She wanted to know his reaction so she told him about the scrap of letter she had found, and Corinne's photograph.

His good spirits left him. 'What have you done with them?'

'I threw the letter away,' she told him. 'But I kept the photo. Would you like it?'

For a moment he didn't reply. He drained his glass and made for the front door.

'No, burn it,' he said sharply.

She hurried after him. 'I can't do that. She's dead. Surely there's a relative who might like it.'

'There are no relatives!'

'Are you sure?'

He turned on her, his grey eyes like slate. 'I told you to burn it. I don't want to see it, do you understand?'

The fierceness in his gaze reminded her of the first time they had met. This time it frightened her.

'Yes, yes, I understand,' she replied hesitantly.

His manner softened slightly. 'Then, please do as I ask.'

He opened the front door and left without repeating the kiss he had given her in the car. She watched him drive off and went back into the cottage with a flat feeling of disappointment. It was her own fault, she told herself. She had ruined everything by deliberately alluding to the other girl.

★ ★ ★

Through the rest of the evening her disappointment stayed with her. Over and over again she wished she'd kept the photograph a secret.

She went upstairs and fetched it, studying the girl who looked back at her until she felt as though she had known her personally. Then she burnt it in the old-fashioned fireplace as Sebastian had asked.

The shiny paper caught fire and curled up. The other girl's eyes met hers challengingly, seeming to tell her that although she was dead Sebastian would always belong to her.

When the paper had blackened, Albany prodded it with the poker so that it crumbled into ash. Then she looked up quickly in the direction of the window. The curtains were undrawn. For a second she thought she had caught sight of someone standing there watching her. The feeling was so strong that she went to look out.

There was no one there now, but a shadow fell across the ground where the light over the front door shone down. Albany drew in her breath.

'Who's there?' she called out.

No one answered, and rather than open the front door Albany ran lightly upstairs and looked out of her bedroom window.

The shadow below had moved. But as she looked further along the drive she could see the figure of a woman. Albany stood transfixed. Slowly the woman turned and looked directly up at her.

Putting her hand up to her mouth, Albany stifled a cry of terror. The woman had the face of Corinne Latour!

6

While Albany watched, the woman turned away again and the darkness in the drive seemed to swallow her up. Drawing courage Albany told herself she must have imagined it all. The face in the photograph had transfixed itself in her mind. If there had been a person in the drive at all, it was certainly not Corinne Latour. The last tenant of the cottage was dead: drowned whilst taking a swim at Hunters Cove.

She went to bed and read until her eyes ached, then fell into a restless sleep, haunted by dreams of Miles and Sebastian holding Corinne's head under the water until she went limp and finally turned into a large fish.

She woke with a start to find it was almost half past eight. She remembered her first appointment was at half past nine.

Just before she left the cottage Rose, who helped at the Manor, came to see her.

'Mr Blaire said I should call to find out when you'd like me to come in and clean for you,' she said in her attractive country accent.

Albany invited her in. She and Rose were about the same age. But the other young woman was married with two small children.

'I don't know how on earth you find the time to go out to work,' Albany remarked, offering her a cup of coffee, which she refused. 'Who does *your* housework while you're out doing other people's?'

Rose laughed. 'Oh, I don't have any, more's the pity. I live with mother-in-law, my husband being in the Navy and away at sea most of the time. So she looks after the kiddies and cleans the place while I go out to work.' She gave a shrug. 'It's the best way really, rather than be at home all the time — two women in the same house, sharing the same kitchen, squabbling over what the kids are up to. It doesn't really work.'

Albany nodded without making any comment. She had hardly spoken to Rose before but had always considered her an intelligent person, too intelligent for such a dead-end occupation as doing other people's housework all day long.

'Well, I'm very grateful you're going to take some of the household tasks off my hands,' she said. 'Sebastian Blaire suggested three afternoons a week: perhaps Mondays, Wednesdays and Fridays? Would that be all right? I expect you're busy at the Manor in the mornings?'

'Yes, miss, that's right. Mrs Blaire likes me to get up to the house in time to make breakfast for her. She's a late riser. Generally gets downstairs about ten o'clock. I'm there Mondays to Fridays from half past nine to half past twelve as a rule, unless anyone wants me to help with dinner parties. But there's few enough of those these days. So, if you like, I can come here from two till five each of those three days. Will that suit?'

Albany thanked her. 'Indeed it will! Does that mean you'll be starting this afternoon?'

Rose gave a nod. 'Why yes, if you like. Today's Friday, after all.'

'Then I'd better let you have a key. I've a patient the other side of Petersville I have to treat during their lunchtime, which means I may not be back till after three. Usually my father will be about but he's in hospital at the moment.'

'Oh, I'm really sorry to hear that, miss. He and I get on a treat. He's an extremely nice, quiet sort of gentleman. Sometimes I help him to choose Mr Blaire's books to read. A lot of the ones he likes are on the top shelves, too difficult for him to reach.'

'Then you'll be pleased to learn he's only in hospital for a check-up. I shall be bringing him home again tomorrow.'

Rose looked pleased. 'I'm very relieved to hear that.'

A disturbing thought struck Albany. 'Did you say my father's been borrowing Mr Blaire's books in the Manor library?'

'Why, yes, miss.'

'How long has that been going on? Since before Mr Blaire came back?'

'Goodness me, yes.'

Albany grew worried. 'I only hope Mr Blaire hasn't objected.'

'I don't think he'd do that, Miss Edmunds. He's not like that. I'm sure if Mrs Blaire gave your father permission in the first place he wouldn't go back on it.'

Albany found herself thinking that Olivia Blaire seemed to take a lot on herself for a guest in someone's house. Especially since she had given the impression she was not all that keen on her step-son.

She gave a glance at the sitting room clock. 'I shall have to leave now if you don't mind.'

'I'd better wake my ideas up, too,' said Rose. 'I'll be late cooking Mrs Blaire's breakfast if I'm not careful.'

Albany handed Rose a set of keys to the cottage and then remembered about the person whom she thought she had seen in the drive the night before.

'Oh, by the way — you didn't help out with dinner at the Manor last night, did you? I think they had a visitor.'

'No, miss. I haven't helped out with dinners there for more than twelve months. Not since Mr Blaire and Miss Latour used to hold a few parties for their friends.' She paused delicately. 'She was the young woman who used to live here before you, the one who got drowned at Hunters Cove. I expect you've been told.'

Albany nodded. 'Yes, a very sad thing.'

'Oh, it was. I didn't think Mr Blaire would ever get over it. But time heals everything in the end.'

'I'm sure you're right,' Albany agreed,

closing the door behind them. 'Goodbye, Rose. I might see you later this afternoon.'

★ ★ ★

Time seemed to drag for Albany that morning. Crowded into her thoughts was her impatience to see Sebastian again. Repeatedly she told herself what a fool she had been to bring up the subject of the dead girl, especially after witnessing Sebastian's reaction at the potter's. How different things might have been between them if only she had kept the existence of the photograph to herself.

It was with a feeling of relief that she drove home after treating her last patient for the day. Uppermost in her mind was the hope that Sebastian might call again.

After she put her car in the garage she spied Rose at the window straightening the bedroom curtains. When Albany went upstairs Rose was just putting the finishing touches to her room. Albany took off her white overall and folded it neatly over the back of a chair.

'I don't know how we managed before you came,' she remarked. 'The place would have gone to rack and ruin.'

'I doubt that, miss,' Rose said with a shake of her head. 'You're not the sort of person to neglect a house.'

'I merely do what's necessary and that's all.' An inquisitive thought occurred to Albany. 'Did you clean the cottage when Corinne Latour lived here?'

'No, one of the other housemaids did. But she's left now. I used to come in occasionally when she was on holiday.'

'Did Miss Latour work locally?'

Rose frowned. 'I don't believe she worked at all. She used to go out quite a bit. She was French, very beautiful. I used to think she'd been a model at some time.'

'How long did she live here?'

'She came about six months before Mr Blaire. That was in Major Royal's time — he sold the Manor to Mr Blaire.' She smiled. 'Curious, wasn't it, that this should be called Blaire Manor? Maybe that's what encouraged Mr Blaire to buy it. Oh, by the way, Jefferson's brought along a great bunch of red roses from the Manor gardens. I put them in that huge glass vase in the sitting room. I hope that was right. They looked lovely there, just as though it was bought specially for them.'

Albany went downstairs quickly.

The sight of the velvet beauty of the dark red roses brought a spontaneous smile to her lips. As Rose had said, it looked just as though it had been bought specially to hold them. For a moment she dared to wonder. Was it possible Sebastian had bought the vase just so that he could give her flowers?

The thought was too ridiculous to contemplate. She was blowing up the peck on the cheek he had given her out of all proportion, like Miles' new receptionist!

All the same, she had an overwhelming desire to see him again, even if it was purely on friendly terms. She had been going to use her father's borrowing of his books as an excuse. But now the roses would give her an added reason.

Half way up to the Manor she regretted her hasty decision. What if he guessed the real reason for her visit? After all, she could easily have thanked him over the phone.

She took longer to cover the last few yards, hesitating when she reached the front door, wondering whether to ring the bell or turn tail without anyone seeing her. Then, through the partly open sitting room window she heard the raised voices of Sebastian and his step-mother.

'You're a cruel, vindictive person, Sebastian. You know very well I can't find anywhere else to live.'

Sebastian's voice interrupted, sharp with anger.

'I told you when I first came back that I wanted you out within seven days. That time's long elapsed. I suppose you thought I'd forgotten about it, or that I'd reconsidered?'

'I thought nothing of the sort, knowing you. But I haven't been able to find anywhere else — at least nothing of the kind I've grown used to.'

His tone was scathing. 'Then it's time you lowered your sights. It won't harm you to adjust to less-extravagant living. I won't foot your bills any longer!'

'But you've got the whole of this beautiful Manor. Surely you could allow me to live in one of the wings?'

'That I own this place is no thanks to you. I'll give you to the middle of next week. If you're not out by then I shall personally pack your things and hurl them out of the front door!'

Albany didn't stay to hear any more. She hurried back along the drive as though his words had been meant for *her* and not his step-mother.

106

Sebastian in a temper, as far as she was concerned, was not a person to be treated lightly. There would be another time to thank him for the roses.

★ ★ ★

When Rose left at five, Albany debated whether she should stay in the cottage by herself all evening, or whether she should treat herself to a meal in the seaside town of Weymouth some miles away. The latter seemed more inviting than spending another evening there alone.

The drive took her about half an hour. When she arrived she put her car in the car park and took a walk along the promenade. It was interesting to watch the summer visitors making the most of every moment of their holidays, many still on the beach and in the water, although the evening was growing cooler.

Walking the length of the promenade as far as the sand sculptures, she strolled back again until she came to Greenhill gardens. It was there, seeing inside the window of a brightly lit cafe, that she suddenly realised she hadn't eaten anything since early that day.

She entered and chose a window seat where she could look out over the sea. It was growing dusk and twinkling lights had come on along the promenade. A large moon sailed across the sky.

When her meal finally came, she found she did not really want it. She stared out thoughtfully at carefree couples strolling arm in arm, feeling a mixture of jealousy and dejection. Why, oh, why had she told Sebastian about that photograph?

She was wallowing in 'if onlys' when a voice she knew broke the spell.

'Hey, Albany Edmunds! What a coincidence *you* being in Weymouth on our first evening here. I was going to get in touch with you tomorrow.'

She looked up to see her old schoolfriend smiling down at her. By her side were two young children.

'Rachel Robinson!' She smiled back. 'Sorry, it's no good — I shall always go on thinking of you by your single name.'

'Do you mind if we join you?' the overweight young woman said, plumping herself gratefully into a chair by her side. The two children scrambled up onto chairs opposite. 'I brought Bobbie and Beverley out for a quick look at the sea before I put them to bed. Robert's propping up the bar at the hotel where we're staying.'

'You promised us an ice-cream, mummy!' the children reminded her.

'So I did.'

'Let me get them,' Albany offered, beckoning to the busy waitress. 'Coffee for you, Rachel, or would you like something else?'

'Coffee, black, although I hate it,' the other woman said making a face. 'I promised Doctor Sheering I'd lose two stones before I saw him again. I don't know *how* I'm going to do it.'

'How's the back?' Albany asked sympathetically.

'A lot better since you treated it. But I must admit I find the exercises a job to fit in, especially now we're on holiday.'

'You can do them on the beach!'

'What, in a swimsuit?'

'Why not?'

'Albany, finding a swimsuit in my size, let alone having the courage to put it on, is a work of art.'

'Nonsense, there are plenty of shops that cater for larger sizes.'

Rachel sighed. 'Let's hope I won't be 'larger sized' for long. I've promised myself by hook or by crook I'll lose weight this time. If I don't, I shall have Robert looking elsewhere.'

Albany smiled. 'I don't believe you.'

'Well,' the other woman admitted. 'Perhaps I'm exaggerating slightly. But do you realise I'd crash-dieted down to a sylphlike eight stone before I got married and now I'm . . . ' she paused and gave a glance at her daughter who was listening with interest. 'No, I'm not going to say. It'll be all over Beverley's kindergarten otherwise. She's turning into a real little gossip.'

The overworked waitress hurried over with the coffee and ice-creams and Rachel steered the conversation round to Albany.

'What are you doing at the seaside all on your own, anyway? And how are you getting on at Drive Cottage?'

'We love it. But father had to go back to Bridesmay for a check-up and I didn't fancy spending another evening there all on my own.'

'All on your own! I'm surprised at you, Albany. Haven't you found a boyfriend yet?'

'No time! Doctor Planter from the village has kindly put a lot of referrals my way, so most of my time is divided between treating patients and looking after father.'

'You know what they say about all work and no play! But how about this Doctor Planter? I went to see him about Beverley's cough the last time I visited Robert's Aunt Olivia. If I remember rightly, he was what one might call tall, fair and very comely.'

Albany admitted reluctantly, 'I went sailing with him once, but it was on purely friendly terms.'

'On yours but not on his, if my instinct tells me right.' When Albany made no comment the other woman went on: 'Which reminds me, Aunt Olivia asked us to call in while we're down. She mentioned her step-son had just returned home. Have you had the chance to meet him yet?'

'Well, yes.'

Rachel egged her on. 'Go on — what's he *really* like? Olivia's always given us the impression he's a bit of a bast — whoops, not in front of the children! Anyway, a kind of super brat, a spoilt daddy's boy.'

Albany found herself defending him hotly. 'He's nothing like that. He's generous and kind.'

'Really! I thought he couldn't be *too*

bad, since Olivia said he encouraged her to sell her house and go and live at Blaire Manor while he was abroad.'

Albany found herself recalling the argument she had overheard.

'Tell me, what do you know about Olivia? Have you known her very long?'

'I hardly know her at all. She's not my side of the family. Robert's talked a bit about her. Apparently, she was a bit of a tearaway when she was younger — went against the family's wishes and became an actress. Not a very good one, I imagine, since she got into all kinds of scrapes over money and earned herself a reputation. Then the next thing is she's married to Colonel Blaire and spending *his* money instead of her own.'

The children interrupted, having finished their ice-creams and grown restless.

'You promised us a paddle before we went back.'

Rachel gulped down the last of her coffee and got up.

'So I did. It's almost pitch dark now. Look, Albany, why don't we get together one day while I'm here? Robert can take a turn at child-minding and I'll drive over.'

'Fine, how about Tuesday? No, make it Wednesday and I'll have less patients.'

'Quite a career girl.' Rachel scrutinised her. 'You must be finding it a bit of job to look after your father and carry on with your work. You're looking thinner than when I saw you last, damn you! Anyway, give your father my love. See you Wednesday.'

Albany watched them go, Rachel waddling to keep up with the children. She startled herself by her slight feeling of envy. Rachel might be severely overweight, but at least she had a purpose in life, a husband and children. Insurance against a lonely old age! What had *she* got? She was nearly thirty and where was she going?

She pulled herself together. Goodness, anyone would think she was pushing *forty* the way she was complaining. She had excellent qualifications and an enviable career. It was true that at the moment she seemed to be marking time. But that was because she was looking after father. *Her* time would come.

She tried to hold on to that thought as she went in search of her car.

7

The next morning, when Albany arrived at the hospital near Oxford, the first person she went to see was the doctor in charge of her father's case. She had known the swarthy skinned Asian doctor and his family for a number of years.

He gave her a warm smile as his secretary showed her in.

'Hello, Albany. I've been looking forward to seeing you. We're very pleased with your father, and it's all due to you.'

'Oh, no,' she said, disagreeing modestly.

'Oh, yes! Besides getting him stronger physically you've given him a reason for living. Instead of staying here, where you stood a good chance of being made head of your department, you took him away where he could start afresh. Without that it would have taken much longer for him to acclimatise to life without his wife, let alone greatly restricted movement. As it is, I think we can safely cut his visits down to four-monthly. Which means you can bring him back to see us again around Christmas. You can arrange the exact date with the receptionist.'

She thanked him, then saw him give a furtive look at his watch, which told her how busy he was. She started to leave. But he called her back.

'However, that doesn't mean he's going to need spoon-feeding till then, Albany. It might be a good idea to let him have more freedom.'

She looked surprised.

'Why not set him loose in the nearest town so that he can make friends and become less reliant on you?'

'But we're several miles even from the nearest village!'

He laughed. 'Goodness me, you're really out in the sticks! Haven't you thought about claiming an invalid car

117

for him? You know, one of these days you're going to start wanting your independence back.' He became more serious, his liquid brown eyes searching hers. 'It's very easy to become a martyr and start blaming someone else at the back of your mind for depriving you of what's rightly yours, the chance to marry and have children.'

His words, too close to the truth for comfort, made her feel indignant but she tried not to show it.

'Very well. I'll put it to him and see what he says about a car.'

He smiled kindly. 'Yes, I should, Albany.'

Later, when they were driving home, she broached the subject to her father tentatively.

'How would you feel about having a car of your own to drive around in like you used to?'

He gave her an odd look. 'Tired of being my chauffeur already?'

She felt guilty. 'No, of course not. But there must be times when you'd like to slip into town while I'm out treating a patient. You'd be able to use the public library instead of treating Sebastian's house like one.'

'I rather like his choice of books. They happen to coincide with my own.'

She sighed. 'You're just being awkward. Anyway, did he say you could borrow them? I was under the impression you were borrowing Olivia's.'

'I was to begin with. But I got tempted when I saw all the rows and rows of travel books. And Olivia said it would be quite in order.'

'We thought that about the agreement, if you remember,' she said pointedly.

'So we did. All right, what kind of car shall I have, a Rolls Royce or a Bentley?'

'I'll make enquiries at the local Social Security office,' she promised. 'I think you'll quite enjoy having your independence back, instead of having to rely on me all the time.'

He smiled as he glanced at her serious profile, thinking how very much he owed to her unselfish nature. He would never let her know that it had been *he* who had put the idea of an invalid car in Doctor Bhazi's head. He wouldn't dream of hurting her for the world. Nor would he deprive her of her life.

The first thing he noticed when they got home was the cut glass vase filled with red roses.

'What's this, 'Welcome Home Father'? I bet that set you back a bit.'

'It's an offering from Sebastian Blaire.'

'For me or for you?'

She felt herself growing embarrassed. 'For the cottage, I suppose. He's within his rights to put ornaments in it.'

Darrel wasn't slow in catching her heightened colour. But he let it pass. 'Well, yes, I suppose so.'

'Oh, by the way,' she said quickly to get away from the subject, 'I've altered your bedroom around. I don't think the moon will shine in on your face any more.'

'That looks fine,' he commented, wheeling himself in to see. 'It looks as though you've been busy. I haven't seen the furniture shining as brightly as this since we first moved in.'

She shrugged. 'I can't claim the praise for that, I'm afraid. Rose from the Manor is coming in to clean for us three times a week.'

'And a very good idea, too. But you're not to pay her out of your fees. I'll settle with Miss Rosie.'

'Too late,' she said, hiding her expression. 'Sebastian Blaire is settling it. It comes in with the rent we pay. He was surprised to learn it hadn't already been arranged.'

'Was he, indeed? And have you been seeing very much of each other while I was away?' He tried to make the question sound offhand.

'No, not very much.'

He was quick to catch her faraway look but didn't pursue the matter.

'What say we have a spot of lunch at the local, instead of you getting it ready?' he suggested. 'I haven't forgotten you're going sailing with Miles Planter this afternoon.'

She left the room hurriedly. 'No, I'm not. I've put it off. He wasn't very pleased about it, as a matter of fact.'

'I bet he wasn't.'

'Anyway, lunch is all prepared. I've only got to shove it in the oven.'

★ ★ ★

Over the next few days Albany hardly caught sight of Sebastian. She thought he was probably avoiding her and the idea made her miserable. Then, unexpectedly, on the Monday evening she saw him walking down the drive towards her and her legs turned to jelly.

She went back to close the gates after putting her car away and he caught her up.

'Working late this evening,' he commented.

'It's necessary sometimes,' she murmured.

'Why's that?'

She told him. 'Sometimes my patients have to go out during the day. Since they're paying the piper I have to fit my times in with theirs.'

'Oh, is that one of the reasons you preferred working in the clinic?'

'Not really.' She caught him studying her expression and grew tongue-tied. 'Where are you off to, anyway? I didn't know you were in the habit of taking moonlight strolls.'

'I'm not.' He closed the heavy gates for her.

'You're not going any further then?' she asked in surprise.

'No. I only intended coming as far as the cottage. That's enough for an unaccustomed constitutional.'

'Why do it at all if you're not keen on it?'

'Why, indeed? What would you say

if I told you I'd done it on purpose, hoping I'd bump into you?'

She put a hand to her cheek, involuntarily.

'Don't look so surprised,' he chided. 'I've had you on my mind a lot just lately. You've been quite a distraction. I came down on purpose to discuss this state of affairs with you.'

The matter-of-fact way in which he said it took away her joy.

'I'm pretty much a loner, Albany,' he went on. 'I've been in love just once in my lifetime, and I'm not sure I've got that time out of my system yet.'

'You're talking about Corinne Latour?'

'Yes, Corinne.'

'Were you very deeply in love?'

'Yes, I was.'

Her disappointment deepened. 'Then I imagine you still are.'

He threw back his head and laughed. When the laughter died he looked down at her. She could sense a wildness and suppressed agony in his expression that she had never seen there before. It made her heart ache.

'In that case I can't see why you say I'm a distraction to you,' she said softly. 'In my experience, a person can only have one other person on their mind at a time.'

He took her by the shoulders. She could feel his strong grip through her thin coat.

'It's quite clear you don't understand. And why should I tell you?'

She looked back, searching his eyes. It was then he took her by surprise. Dipping his face to hers, he kissed her lightly at first, then with a growing hunger, gathering her slender body against his as soon as he found his kiss returned. For several blissful moments Albany was content to let their embrace take its course, knowing it was what she had longed for ever since their first meeting.

When he released her she found she was shivering. Without speaking they walked together back to the cottage.

At the door he kissed her once more, this time less passionately. Then he stood back, the corners of his mouth lifting as he smiled.

'At least I've found out one thing from my unaccustomed constitutional,' he said wryly.

'And what's that?' she asked.

'I flatter myself I might have been on your mind, too.'

She refused to give him the satisfaction of hearing it from her. Why should she, when the ghost of Corinne lay between them? Her fingers sought the handle of the door. She was about to open it without replying, when he grasped her wrist and stopped her.

'At least let me know whether I'm right, Albany.'

'Why?' she asked stiffly. 'So that you can feel at liberty to steal my kisses whenever the fancy takes you?'

He studied her anger before freeing her.

'If I stole them then I'm sorry. But, believe me, I was under the impression the pleasure was mutual.'

Her eyes flashed.

'Then you have a lot to learn, Mr Blaire.' She shut the door swiftly before he had a chance to reply.

In bed that night Albany tried to justify her harsh treatment of Sebastian. She knew it was jealousy because he had as good as admitted that his love for Corinne was still alive. All she was to him was a mild distraction. That could mean anything.

The pain of being so much in love caused her to lie awake for a long time reliving their kiss. But it was in a bitter-sweet way, knowing it could never be repeated. If she could not have Sebastian to herself completely, she did not want him at all. There could be no half measures as far as she was concerned.

She realised now, for the first time in her life, that it was in her nature to be passionate and possessive. It was probably the reason she had never allowed herself to fall so deeply in love before. But her father had known. He'd told her that when she found the man who was going to set her heart on fire it would be a different thing altogether. And it was. Oh, it was!

8

When Rachel turned up the following Wednesday afternoon the weather was so fine it seemed a shame to waste it by staying indoors. Darrel Edmunds had joined a club for other disabled in the area and had gone on a coach outing.

'Shall we take a walk down to Hunters Cove?' Albany asked. 'It's only about a mile away across the fields. Or would you prefer to take a stroll in the grounds?'

'Whichever's the least taxing,' Rachel replied, pushing her lank hair away from her forehead. 'It's all right for you with your fairy figure, but the heat of the last few days has been getting to me. I feel every step I take will be my last. I'm positively melting.'

Albany smiled. 'You're exaggerating as usual. But if you really can't face the

129

walk, we'll take the longer way round in the car instead.'

'Oh, good. And you can do the driving because then I can take my shoes off. They're killing me.'

Albany shook her head. 'I really shouldn't be aiding and abetting you to avoid exercise. But since you're on holiday I won't preach.'

'No, you'd better not. I get enough of that from Robert and Doctor Sheering.' She kicked off her shoes and sprawled heavily in the passenger seat the moment Albany got her car out of the garage.

They stopped outside the pub at Hunters Cove where Albany had parked the day Sebastian had met her on the jetty. The thought of him brought a heaviness to her heart. She had only managed to catch sight of him once since the night he had kissed her. Their relationship seemed to have slipped back to square one again.

She tried to buoy herself up with the thought that at least she had kept her dignity. If she had meant anything more to him than a minor distraction, he would surely have made some effort to see her, even if it had meant reverting to subterfuge in order to save his face. But it was evident she was no longer on his mind.

Rachel consented to a short stroll along the jetty, agreeing more because the water made her feel cool than because she wanted to please her friend.

When they reached the place where Miles Planter usually moored his boat, Albany was surprised and slightly embarrassed to find him there working on the motor. If it had been possible she would have tried to pass by without him seeing her, but Rachel made that out of the question.

'Why, Doctor Planter, we meet again!' She stopped to lean heavily against a bollard, grinning down at him. 'I doubt if you remember me — Rachel Travers. I brought little Beverley to see you some months ago

When I was visiting my aunt at Blaire Manor.'

Miles threw her a quick glance before focussing his gaze on Albany, tossing her a challenging smile. She could see his eyes taking in the fact that she was dressed only briefly in a pale yellow tee shirt and well-cut shorts. She was not to know that in his estimation she made the other woman look even more dowdy and overweight.

'Yes, of course I remember you.' His eyes remained on Albany. 'Are you staying in the district? Or is this just another short visit?'

'A short visit,' Rachel told him. 'Albany and I are old schoolfriends.'

He raised his eyebrows. 'Is that so?' He didn't add that Albany looked at least ten years her junior. 'How about you, Albany? No patients today?'

She shook her head. 'I kept today free. I shall make up for it tomorrow.'

His smile grew slightly insolent. 'Don't think you have to account to me for it. You're free to work whatever hours you want. I merely provide you with the patients.'

She coloured. 'I'm well aware of that and in spite of — I mean, whatever you may think, I'm extremely grateful.'

He used her gratitude to twist her arm. 'I'm glad to hear that because I need a spot of assistance with the *Merry Lark*. I've been fixing her motor, she'd been a bit sluggish. Would you and your friend like to come for a quick sail while I try it out? I may need you to take the helm.'

'Oh, bliss!' Rachel said rapturously, levering herself down over the side of the jetty, causing the yacht to sink lower in the water. 'I can't think of anything I'd like better on a warm day like today. Can I wallow in the bow and paddle my hands in the water?'

'Feel free to wallow wherever you like as long as you're not afraid of the odd basking shark,' he joked.

Albany remained on the jetty a moment longer, angry at the shallow pretext he'd used to get her on board.

If it had not sounded so offensive she would have refused. But Rachel was already there making herself at home and it would have looked churlish on her part. There was nothing for it but to grit her teeth against the unnecessary way Miles held her close to him as he assisted her on board and make the best of things. After she had managed to extricate herself he made a playful grab for her again.

'Watch out! Can't have you falling over the side. What would happen to your dear old ladies then? Not to mention a certain young man who lives at the Manor?'

'What on earth has Albany falling overboard got to do with Sebastian?' Rachel asked in a mystified voice. 'I suppose you realise he's a sort of cousin of mine.'

He laughed. 'You'll have to get Albany to unburden her heart to you sometime since you're old school-friends. I understand that's what schoolgirls used to do, swap stories about their secret passions!'

'Oh, do be quiet, Miles, otherwise you can keep your stupid boat trip,' Albany told him furiously. 'Just tell me where you want me to steer her.'

'Out of the harbour might be a good way. And then anywhere from there. Though it might be a nice idea to sail round to Lyme Regis.'

'That's far too far,' Albany snapped.

'I don't think so at all,' Rachel said lazily.

'Guests are always right — Lyme Regis it is,' said Miles heartily.

Outnumbered, Albany did her best to stay out of Miles' way for the rest of the trip. But it was difficult on such a small boat. Fortunately, from then onwards, he behaved like a perfect gentleman, making no further attempt to bate her, and treating them to tea at a harbourside cafe when they arrived at their destination.

They arrived back at Hunters Cove in the early evening. Rachel gushed over him as he helped them on to the jetty.

'What a wonderful time you've given us. Far nicer than the stroll round the harbour Albany had planned for me. Really, I sometimes think she has no imagination. And the tea was gorgeous, too. Even if I *did* have an extra cream bun. But I'm sure breathing in all that sea air got rid of a load of calories. So I don't have to worry too much.'

'It was nice having you on board again, Albany,' Miles said wistfully, ignoring Rachel's empty flow. His expression was serious for once. 'Maybe we can repeat it in the not too distant future.'

'I'll think about it,' she said, more to get away from him without a fuss than because she really meant it.

'Yes, do that.' He added for her ears only: 'It's silly to fall out.'

On the way home Rachel could talk of nothing else but the good-looking doctor. Albany grew a little tired of her. Her behaviour during the afternoon had often been annoying. She remembered that they had never been exactly close friends when they were at school. It was the reason they had not kept in touch.

'Oh, how I wish I could take him home with me!'

'What on earth for?' asked Albany, surprised. 'I thought you were in love with Robert.'

'Of course I am, but sometimes he's abominably inattentive. Having Miles around might make him buck up his ideas and stop taking me for granted.'

As Rachel waffled on, often talking for the sake of talking, a seed was planted in the back of Albany's mind. Maybe she could turn Miles' regard for her to good advantage. If Rachel was so sure it would make Robert jealous, it could do the same thing for Sebastian, provided he felt anything for her at all. She would work on it for a future date.

'Something Miles said has been nagging at me,' Rachel said suddenly.

'What's that?'

'That curious thing about Sebastian when he was talking about you falling overboard. What did he mean?'

Albany kept her eyes glued to the road ahead.

'I can't think. Miles says a lot of silly things.'

She felt Rachel studying her. 'I know it got you a bit hot round the collar at the time. It must have had a meaning, surely?'

'If it did,' Albany replied, non-committally, 'I can't think of one now.'

Just as they came in view of the drive gates, she saw Sebastian's Porsche streak out, heading in the opposite direction. He had not bothered to close the gates behind him and was driving dangerously fast. She wondered what had happened to make him so foolhardy.

When they arrived at the cottage she saw another car parked outside as well as Rachel's Rover and recognised it as Olivia Blaire's blue Opel. Father had evidently returned from his outing and Olivia had stopped to chat with him.

Rachel spotted the car at the same moment.

'Doesn't that belong to my aunt? I hope so. It'll save me the bother of going up to see her.' She glanced at her watch. 'I daren't stay too much longer. Robert will be going spare looking after the children all afternoon.'

When Rachel got out, Albany drove her car straight into the garage. She stayed behind just long enough to settle her car down for the night before following the other women into the house. Even before she reached the sitting room she heard the sound of loud sobbing and wondered what was the matter.

As she went in it became clear. Olivia Blaire had collapsed in an armchair. Her face was buried in her hands and she was weeping noisily. Darrel Edmunds was sitting in his wheelchair on the other side of the room looking awkward. The moment he saw Albany he exclaimed in a relieved tone: 'Thank goodness you're here. I was beginning to get out of my depth.'

'What's the matter?'

'I've no idea,' he whispered. 'I've been trying to get it out of her for the last quarter of an hour, but it seems all she can do is make that awful noise. I was nearly at my wits' end. I was thinking about ringing for Miles or his partner.'

Rachel had already put her large, comforting arms around the sobbing woman and was talking to her sympathetically.

'What's the matter, auntie? It's Rachel. I was just about to come and see you but you're here instead. Whatever's upset you? Surely you can tell us about it.'

'Oh, I can't, I can't! It's too terrible to talk about. I can't tell anyone, I can't tell anyone at all.'

'But you've got to. You can't go on

crying like this, you'll make yourself ill.'

'Oh, I *am* ill, my dear. It's enough to make anyone ill the trauma I've been through.'

'Then you've got to tell us about it. What is it? Has someone attacked you?'

The woman refused to reply, sobbing more violently than ever.

'Come on, Aunt Olivia. You've *got* to tell us. Has someone broken into the Manor and attacked you?'

'Oh, I can't talk about it. I really can't talk about it!'

Albany remembered the breakneck speed Sebastian had been travelling coming out of the drive.

'Is that what happened?' she asked kindly. 'Has Sebastian gone out to find them?'

Olivia's voice rose to a pitiful wail. 'Oh, don't mention that name to me. Don't ever mention that name to me again!'

Albany looked at her father for

support. Surely the way the woman was behaving could not have anything to do with Sebastian?

'There must be some mistake,' she said.

'There's no mistake,' the woman sobbed. 'That revolting step-son of mine has threatened me with a rifle. He told me if I wasn't packed and out of his house within an hour he'd use it on me. Of course, I didn't even wait to pack a thing. I just left, in fear of my life, and came straight here. Fortunately Darrel had just arrived home and I threw myself on his mercy.'

Albany could hardly believe her ears. 'You say Sebastian threatened you with a gun?'

Olivia looked up. Her eyes, though slightly red, showed no sign of tears or ravaged eye make-up.

'Isn't that what I've just said? He waved a rifle in the air at me like this, and said he'd kill me if I wasn't out of his house within half an hour!'

'You said an hour?'

'An hour, half an hour! What does it matter? The man's gone raving mad. I tell you, I left in fear of my life.' She lapsed into noisy sobs again. 'Where can I go, what can I do? I daren't go back to the house on my own. But I haven't packed a thing. It'll take me days to pack all my expensive furs and dresses, not to mention my jewellery, and, and, so many other little comforts!'

Albany remembered the heated exchange between Olivia and Sebastian that she had tried to put out of her mind until now.

She tested the woman's honesty. 'Did Sebastian give you any reason for wanting you to leave?'

'No, none at all. It just happened out of the blue. We had never so much as discussed it before. And then, suddenly, there he was confronting me with a gun and telling me to get out!'

'Hadn't he perhaps mentioned he'd

like the Manor to himself, and given you a time limit?'

'What do you mean?' Olivia's sobbing came to an abrupt halt. She glared at Albany. 'Are you accusing me of telling lies? Isn't it enough that I've had to humiliate myself by coming here and revealing my circumstances?' Her voice grew more indignant. 'How would *you* feel if someone you'd tried to be a mother to suddenly brandished a rifle in your face and told you to get out within five minutes?'

'An *hour*, auntie. You're overwrought.' Rachel came to her rescue. 'Anyway there's no question of you going up to the Manor and collecting your things. Albany and I will go. And I shall have the pleasure of telling Sebastian exactly what I think of him.'

'But what shall I do? I've nowhere to go, even when I get my things out of the house.' Olivia looked all set to start sobbing again.

Rachel smiled indulgently. 'Why, you'll come back to Weymouth with me, of course. Robert will second that. We'll finish our holiday and then all go home together. You'll have plenty of time to sort yourself out and decide what you want to do.'

Olivia's expression became instantly transformed.

'My dear Rachel! How kind you are. I've always thought that at the back of my mind. I've said to myself on several occasions how nice it would be to live with you. We're all going to be so happy living together, you and me and Robert!'

Rachel's look grew slightly worried. 'You mustn't forget Bobbie and Beverley. It'll mean turning Bobbie out of his room.' She brightened. 'But it'll only be for a while, just until you find somewhere else to live. I've remembered, there are some really nice, one-person flatlets quite close to us.'

Olivia shuddered. 'Oh, no, I don't think they would do at all. I have so many things.'

Rachel's face grew doubtful again. 'Well, we'd better play it by ear, hadn't we? I'll give Robert a ring and let him know what's happened.'

While she was on the phone Albany made some tea for everyone. Her thoughts were jumping. It was clear that everything that had happened had been exaggerated by Olivia. It was impossible to believe Sebastian had threatened her with a rifle. He had probably had it in his hands at the time, perhaps cleaning it, when he had tackled her again about leaving. There had more than likely been another verbal battle between them, and Olivia had driven to the cottage, hoping to throw herself on Darrel's mercy, perhaps even hoping she would be asked to stay. Perish the thought!

She wondered what Olivia had done in the past to merit Sebastian's wrath. She had probably spread insidious rumours about him, as she had had a habit of doing ever since Albany had known her. In view of that it had been generous of Sebastian to allow her to live at the Manor as long as he had.

When she had finished her cup of tea Rachel stood up.

'Come on,' she said to Albany, 'let's get going!'

'Where?' Albany asked in surprise.

'To the Manor, of course, to get some things for Aunt Olivia. We won't be able to collect too much. Just enough to last her a week while we're on holiday. Before we go home Robert and I can come down and collect the rest.'

Albany agreed reluctantly. Foremost in her mind was the thought of what Sebastian would say if he should suddenly arrive home and find them in his house uninvited.

9

Albany and Rachel took Olivia's blue Opel up to the Manor in order to collect her things. It had been agreed she should follow Rachel to Weymouth in her own car for the sake of convenience. Rachel drove, parking in the paved forecourt of the stately mansion. Olivia had provided them with a key to the front door.

Rachel opened it. She put on a brave face. 'Hurry up. Let's get the dastardly deed done as soon as possible. I don't really want a scene with my step-cousin if he should suddenly return. Have you any idea which is her room?'

'None at all,' Albany said nervously. 'We should have asked.'

'Well, it's too bad. We shall just have to go upstairs and search.'

'Don't you think it would be better if you went up on your own?' Albany suggested. 'I'll stay downstairs and keep watch. I'll be able to give you a warning shout if Sebastian puts in an appearance.'

Rachel wasn't taken in. 'Coward!' she said, giving her a withering look. 'Oh, well, since she's *my* relative I suppose I'd better agree. But you'll have to shout loud. The place is as big as Buckingham Palace.'

Albany waited in the hall while Rachel climbed the curved, polished staircase. As soon as she had disappeared she went timidly into the sitting room to keep watch from the large picture window that overlooked the drive.

Really, she thought to herself, the whole thing was like a play, a farce. What sort of defence could she put up if Sebastian came hurtling along the drive while they were still there? If he felt like it he could have them both arrested for breaking and entering. She remembered his angry expression when he thought she was a squatter the first time they met.

Honestly, she had been every kind of an idiot to agree to Rachel's harebrained scheme. She should have had nothing to do with it. But, at the time, it had been easier said than done, with Olivia breaking into hysterics, even though Albany had been practically certain she was only pretending.

She looked around, hating the fact that she was an interloper in someone else's house. It was then that she spied a rifle lying on the seat of a chair. So, at least, Olivia had been telling the truth about *that*. All the same, she refused to believe Sebastian had threatened her with it.

She picked it up tentatively, surprised at how heavy it was. She had never handled a firearm before.

She was getting the feel of it, breaking and locking the barrel and peering through the sights, when she caught the sound of an approaching vehicle. Still with the firearm in her arms she went to the window to look out. Sebastian's dark coloured Porsche was swiftly coming nearer. She stood stock still with fear, forgetting all about the warning shout she had promised Rachel.

She watched him park next to Olivia's Opel before he got out and gave it a fierce glare. Then he came bounding up the steps and into the hall before she knew it.

'All right!' he shouted. 'I know you're in the house somewhere. You'd better come down and face me if you know what's good for you!'

Albany felt the blood draining from her cheeks. Her limbs seemed to have turned to stone. Through the partly open door she could see Sebastian as he paced to the bottom of the stairs. Then he turned and strode into the sitting room.

His angry expression froze the moment he saw her there, the barrel of the rifle she was still holding pointed inadvertently in his direction.

'For God's sake put that thing down!

What the hell do you think you're doing?'

She let it slip. Before it had time to reach the ground, Sebastian had torn over as though making a rugby tackle and managed to catch it.

He placed it back on the chair where he had originally left it.

'What in heaven's name are you doing here, Albany?' he asked in a puzzled tone. 'And where's Olivia? Don't say she's roped you in in an effort to get me to change my mind. Because, if she has, all I can say is that that woman's spent her last night in this house. If I was to reel off a list of all her misdemeanours you'd swear I was exaggerating. That person who calls herself my step-mother has yet to learn the difference between truth and falsehood!'

Albany came back to life, relieved that she had not incurred his wrath by being there.

'Olivia says you threatened her with that gun.'

He looked amused. 'The same way *you* threatened *me* with it just now?'

'That was an accident. I shouldn't have touched it, I'm sorry.'

'But surely you don't believe her story?'

'I don't know what to think. She seemed very upset.'

He shook his head impatiently. 'That woman will distort anything in order to gain sympathy. She was a second-rate actress before she married my father. Does that surprise you?'

'No, I already knew it.'

'Not from *her*?'

'No, from a friend.' Albany gave a gasp. 'Excuse me . . . ' She ran to the bottom of the stairs. 'Rachel, you'd better come down — Sebastian's back!'

He followed her in astonishment. 'And who in the world is Rachel?'

'Rachel's the friend, Olivia's niece. She's collecting some of her things. I was supposed to be keeping my eye open for you.'

His amused look returned but vanished again almost immediately.

'I suppose you realise I could have you both arrested for making free with my house?'

'There was really little else we could do,' she explained awkwardly. 'And you can't accuse us of breaking in since Olivia gave us her key. You couldn't honestly expect her to collect her things herself since you'd succeeded in putting the fear of God into her.'

'Olivia doesn't know what it is to fear God. The only thing she fears is losing her meal ticket.'

'I don't know what you mean,' Albany shrugged. 'And it really isn't any of my business. But I think you could have given her longer than an hour in which to leave.'

'Is that what she told you?' He threw back his head and laughed. 'In point of fact, I've been trying to get her to go for the past month.'

'Even if that's true, I think you could both have behaved with a little more decorum instead of bawling at each other.'

'And how do you know we bawled?' he tackled her.

She decided to tell him the truth. 'Because I came up last week to thank you for the roses, and happened to hear you through the open window.'

He raised an eyebrow sardonically. 'In that case, you know perfectly well I gave her longer than an hour!'

At that moment Rachel started to descend the staircase lugging one of Olivia's suitcases which looked as though it had been filled to the brim. She was taken aback when she saw Sebastian.

'Thanks a lot, Albany,' she said accusingly. 'I thought you were going to shout!'

'I did,' Albany said weakly.

'But not very loud!'

'Actually she has a voice like a foghorn when she's roused.' Sebastian came to her rescue. 'But might I enquire what you're doing here? I hope you haven't packed all the family silver in there. Would you mind hanging on while I telephone for the police?'

In consternation Rachel let the suitcase go and it fell heavily to the bottom of the stairs.

'I can explain everything,' she said, following the suitcase more sedately. 'Though why I should after the way you've treated Aunt Olivia I don't know.'

'Albany tells me I'm supposed to have threatened her with a rifle. I can assure you that's a pack of lies.'

'I suppose you have a witness?' Rachel said, trying to sound knowledgeable.

'It's not up to me to prove I'm telling the truth. It's up to your aunt,' he returned sharply.

'Well, yes, I suppose so,' she admitted uncertainly. 'And actually, she's not *my* aunt, she's my husband's.'

'Is that so? Well, if she's coming to live with you, I wish you great joy of her.' He picked up the suitcase and carried it out to the Opel with them following. 'And a few words of warning: don't forget to check your telephone bill once in a while. She has a habit of ringing friends in Australia and New Zealand when she's feeling lonely. And, oh, yes, I should get in a good supply of oysters and champagne. They happen to be a failing of hers, as I know to my cost. And she also likes to send out Harrod's hampers when friends do her small favours, charged to her benefactor's account, of course. Not to mention expensive little fripperies for herself, like furs, dresses, jewellery and perfume which she has no compunction about having charged to the same account.'

Rachel turned a sickly green.

'None of this is really the truth, is it? You're just trying to put me off having her.'

He shook his head. 'In no way, and I bless you for taking her off my hands. I shall go in and count the cost of the past six months and probably do a little hornpipe as I barricade the front door against her return.'

Albany stared at him, trying hard not to laugh.

He grew serious. 'As a matter of fact, I was getting to the end of my tether. But, since I was fool enough to give in to Olivia's entreaties to come and stay in my absence, I realise I have only myself to blame. I wasn't entirely oblivious to the fact that she's an extremely extravagant person — as well as being a leech. But I sincerely hope you'll be able to unload her again without too much mishap. I've just paid out three months in advance at an hotel in Dorchester. That's the very limit of what I intend doing for her. I'll give it a week before I reclaim the money just to give you a chance. If the going gets tough you can carry her, screaming and shouting blue murder, to *The Royal* in the main street to get her off your back. I can't say fairer than that.'

Rachel glared at him with disbelief before climbing into the driver's seat.

'Come on, Albany, if you're coming. Or do you prefer to stay and listen to some more of his fairy stories? Some people will say anything to get out of trouble.'

Reluctantly Albany obeyed.

'I expect father will be needing me,' she said to Sebastian. 'He's not much good in a crisis.'

He gave a short nod.

'I'm sorry,' she added, 'about giving you such a shock when you got home.'

He smiled. 'The gun wasn't loaded. It fell off the wall when Olivia and I were arguing. I can show you the empty space, if you like. It evidently gave her the idea for her little drama.'

Albany looked surprised. 'Then why the rush to save it when I dropped it?'

He gave a small frown at her stupidity. 'It happens to be quite valuable. It had already had one knock. I didn't want it to have another.'

'Oh, I see.'

Rachel leaned over and slammed

Albany's door forcefully.

'I can't stay here any longer while you two hold a conference. I've an impatient husband and a pair of children waiting for me.'

She started up the car. Sebastian began walking back to the house.

'We'll collect the rest of Aunt Olivia's things later!' Rachel shouted after him.

He didn't bother to reply.

★ ★ ★

The incident of Olivia's departure, which had seemed to bring her and Sebastian closer together, gave Albany new hope. But, at the end of the week, when he'd made no attempt to deepen their relationship, she lost heart.

'What's up with you?' Darrel asked. 'You've been going round like a wet weekend. How about coming for a spin in my new invalid car? We'll go down to the coast. It'll make a change me

160

driving you, instead of the other way about.'

She shook her head dejectedly. 'I've got rather a lot to do in the way of shopping. *You* go down to the coast. It'll do you good to get some more practise in. Would you like me to get you some more books if I find time to pop into the library?'

'No thanks. I haven't finished the last lot yet.'

She smiled, trying to put her own troubles to one side. It was good to see her father looking so much more relaxed. Nice, too, to know he was finding other interests besides reading. Twice a week he went off to his club for the disabled. He was even talking about being invited on to the committee. Soon he'd be out more often than she!

She kissed him goodbye before they each went their separate ways.

The shopping she had to do took a lot less time than she had anticipated. She decided to spin out the afternoon by calling on one of her favourite patients on the way home. It was an old lady called Miss Phipps who lived in the village. She wasn't a private patient, but Miles had referred her to Albany because she found great difficulty getting in to the clinic. Twice a week Albany went to the old lady's cottage to give her heat treatment. But today was to be a social visit since all her equipment was at home.

As she got out and locked her car she happened to glance at the one just in front and recognised it as Miles' white Citroën. At the same moment the old lady's door was opened and Miles let himself out. There was no time for Albany to avoid him.

His face brightened the moment he saw her.

'Surprise, surprise! Long time no see! I've been thinking of giving you a ring but I wasn't sure of my reception.'

Albany was more concerned about Miss Phipps. 'She's all right, isn't she?'

'Who? Oh, Miss Phipps! Yes, right as rain. It was just a routine visit.' He remained looking down at her. 'It's true what I said about not being sure of my reception.' His tone sounded less frivolous than usual. 'I'm not all froth and bubble, you know, Albany. *I* can be hurt just as much as other people.'

She averted her gaze. She didn't feel inclined to be sorry for Miles Planter. She was too busy feeling sorry for herself. Why, oh, why couldn't it have been Sebastian saying these things?

It was just then that she spied him walking towards them, as though the gods had granted her wish. She felt her limbs turn to water. It was the first time she had set eyes on him for days.

'Are you listening to me, Albany?' Miles was going on. 'I'd been thinking of asking you to come sailing with me. Would you, I mean, is it possible to start again where we left off, or is your head still full of Sebastian Blaire?'

She willed herself not to show what she felt.

'Sebastian Blaire? Who's he?' she said in a loud voice.

Miles caught sight of him at the same moment.

'Talk of the devil! I suppose you'd rather I wasn't here?'

'What on earth makes you think that?' she said with what she hoped was an unconcerned shrug. 'You seem to have a bee in your bonnet about me and my landlord.'

He raised his eyebrows in disbelief before giving a grin. 'In that case, I'm not the sort of person to look a gift horse in the mouth. How about coming sailing with me this Saturday?'

Sebastian was close enough to hear Miles' invitation. Albany ignored him as though he wasn't there, making it noticeable she was giving Miles her undivided attention.

'I'd love to! What time?'

'Pick you up at the cottage at two,' he said, sounding pleased.

'Two it is, I'll bring a picnic if you like.'

'Why not? I'll bring a bottle of wine. We should have quite a cosy time.'

It was then she pretended to see Sebastian for the first time.

'Oh, hello,' she said, giving him a distant smile.

Miles threw him a curt nod. 'Hello, Blaire.' Then he glanced at his watch. 'I must get on. See you Saturday, Albany.'

She treated him to the most radiant smile she could muster and he got into his Citroën and drove off.

Albany kept the smile fixed on her face until he was out of sight. Sebastian had stopped at her side. His expression looked baffled.

'Am I to understand you and Miles Planter are going out together?'

She faced him with a slight look of annoyance. 'If it's any business of yours, yes!'

For a moment or two he was silent,

165

studying her upturned gaze. Then he shrugged.

'No, of course it's not any of my business. But I just don't like to see you get hurt. Planter's got quite a reputation. No doubt you've been informed.'

'And there you're quite wrong. I'm well aware of the reputation Doctor Planter *used* to have. But there's no reason why a person shouldn't alter.'

'Leopards don't change their spots, Albany. I'm surprised a grown-up person like you should be so taken-in.'

'How dare you!'

'I dare only because, in spite of what you may think, I still find you a terrific distraction. It's a pity you don't feel the same way about me.'

Her heart wanted to cry out: 'But I do, I do!'

'Nevertheless,' Sebastian was going on, 'I should wear your strongest chastity belt and throw away the key when you go out on the high seas with him on Saturday. Unless, of course, it's seduction you're after.'

Her hand came up and slapped his cheek resoundingly before the sentence was entirely out.

He looked down at her, seeming hardly aware of the blow.

'When I need your advice, Sebastian Blaire, I'll ask for it,' she said tightly, feeling two balls of fiery colour burning her cheeks.

'Any time,' he said with an insolent smile. 'You'll find my bed equally as warm as his.'

10

All the way home, Albany kept thinking of her unexpected meeting with the two men and wondering whether she'd done the right thing. Never in her life had she ever attempted such a despicable trick as playing one person off against another. But it had seemed so opportune at the time, almost as though the fates had planned it, running into Miles like that with Sebastian coming into view at exactly the right moment.

Fortunately, from then until Saturday, she was extremely busy and had little time to regret her action. It was only when the start of the weekend loomed bright with the perfect amount of breeze for sailing that she wished she had refused Miles' invitation. What had she done, raising his hopes like that? She had allowed him to think she was attracted to him and welcomed his attentions, when nothing could be further from her mind. She would hardly be able to blame him if he made a pass.

'Why so thoughtful?' her father asked, coming into the kitchen as she was packing the promised picnic.

'I've done a very silly thing,' she confessed, rinsing four hard-boiled eggs under the tap.

'Do you want to tell me about it?'

'I don't think I'd better. You'd only tell me what a fool I was. And I know that already.'

'Why not try me?'

She heaved a sigh. 'Dad, when you were courting mother did you ever pretend to be interested in someone else so that she'd want you more?'

He gave a small laugh. 'No, that's not the way a man behaves. It's what's known as 'women's wiles'.' He grew more interested. 'Why, is that what you're doing?'

She gave a sad little nod.

'And is it the reason you're going out with Miles Planter this afternoon?'

'Yes,' she admitted in a small voice.

'But he's not the one you'd rather be with?'

She shook her head.

'Then all I can tell you, my girl, is watch yourself. That feller doesn't need a lot of encouragement. If you're egging him on just to make someone else jealous you can't blame him if he tries to take advantage.'

'I know all that. I was hoping for a little sympathy.'

Darrel became kinder. He had already guessed the other person involved.

'I suppose if your surreptitious little plan works, in your estimation it'll be a case of the ends justifying the means.'

She sighed. 'I hope so. I don't really want to hurt anyone. And, at this moment, I'm only hurting myself.'

'Then let this be a lesson to you,' he smiled. 'You're not really the kind of person to play such devious tricks.

I shouldn't try them again.'

'Don't worry, I won't,' she promised.

★ ★ ★

Miles turned up at exactly two o'clock, looking very smart in his casual sailing gear. As Albany went to meet him she found herself thinking that if only she were not so in love with Sebastian she might have found him very attractive.

He got out of his car and gave her a formal, friendly kiss on the cheek. If only he behaves in the same mild way all afternoon, she thought, the day won't be such an ordeal.

Before they left she gave a quick, furtive look round, hoping Sebastian was somewhere near and had seen them, making her scheme worth all its heart searching. But it was then she remembered she had spied his Porsche going out of the gates some while before and not seen it return.

Miles took the picnic bag she was holding and stowed it in the boot.

'It's the perfect day,' he said, getting in beside her. 'And now that you're here with me it's even more perfect.'

His eyes raked hers.

She gave him a small smile, then tried to divert his attention from her by pointing at the sky.

'We'd better be on our way. Isn't that a dark cloud coming up on the horizon?'

'There's no dark cloud on *my* horizon at the moment,' he told her, firing the engine and putting the car in gear. 'But you're right, we'd better get going. There's no knowing when the weather will change.'

On the way to Hunters Cove Albany sat deep in thought.

'Cat got your tongue?' Miles asked playfully.

She had been wondering in a woebegone way where Sebastian had gone. It was plain he did not really care a jot whether she went out with Miles or not. If he had he would have stayed in the Manor grounds and probably

172

followed them from a distance when they left. But she could see he was nowhere in sight. And there was no sign of his Porsche when they stopped near the harbour.

As they took the things from the Citroen and carried them along the jetty to where the *Merry Lark* was bobbing up and down, Albany wondered what the chances were of suddenly feigning violent sickness or a headache in order to get out of the trip. But she knew if she pretended either, Miles would merely tell her he was just as well qualified to treat her *on* board as *off* board. There seemed to be nothing she could do but go ahead and hope she could fend him off if he started getting too amorous.

As Miles undid the mooring rope and they got ready to sail, she looked round desperately once more to see if Sebastian was in sight, perhaps hiding and spying on them. But it was a forlorn thought. In spite of the lovely day there were very few people about, and hardly any boats in the bay. Just one elderly-looking fisherman in a motor dinghy, who, in spite of the sunshine, was wrapped up in yellow oilskins.

She gave a sigh. She was well and truly on her own. She had always believed that people who connived the way she had done got their just desserts. And it looked as though she had got hers. Sebastian had more than likely gone home that day and washed her out of his thoughts. She had probably succeeded in losing any small bit of respect he had ever had for her.

'Why so glum?' Miles asked, perceiving her dejection as he steered the yacht out of the harbour.

She tried to hide it, putting on a smile. 'Who's glum? I often look miserable when I'm thinking.'

'Then stop thinking.' He gave her a gentle squeeze round her waist. 'I'm not averse to dumb blondes.'

She edged away from him. 'I'm not a dumb blonde and I'm a little bit afraid I may have given you the wrong impression. I don't want to get serious about anyone at the moment. I don't intend settling down till I'm at least thirty.'

He gave an amused laugh. 'Who's mentioned anything about settling down? As a matter of fact, I'm glad you told me about that. You know my feelings about getting tied down. I'm the sort of person who likes to have my cake and eat it.'

'Well, I don't,' she said quietly. 'At least, not in the way you mean.'

He raised an eyebrow. 'And how do you know which way I mean?'

'It's obvious. You think I came out with you this afternoon because I want an affair. And I don't.'

He eyed her seriously. 'I don't think you know what you want yet, Albany. I asked you out today so that we could get to know each other a bit better. I enjoy your company. And you — when you're not filling your head full of romantic thoughts about Sebastian Blaire — quite enjoy mine.'

'I told you, I'm not at all interested in Sebastian,' she said quickly.

He shook his head with a little grin. 'You can pull the other one. You didn't fool me one bit the other day, so you can stop congratulating yourself. All the same, I still feel that if we got to know each better you might end up preferring me to him. Or, at least, we could have a steadier sort of relationship. Don't hoodwink yourself into thinking Blaire will be around for much longer. He'll be up and away into the wide blue yonder without a backward wave of his hand as soon as he gets bored. A man without any interests isn't likely to stay anywhere very long in one place.'

What Miles was saying saddened her more than she could say. It was one of the nagging fears she had tried to put to the back of her mind, preferring not to face it. In her heart she knew that Miles was probably speaking the truth. All too soon Sebastian would become bored and leave. He probably would not even take the trouble to inform her. If she was lucky she might get a postcard from him from some distant spot. Maybe he would not be home till the end of another year.

'Let's not ruin our day before it's even begun,' Miles said, sounding sincere. 'If I promise I won't suddenly leap on you, tearing your clothes asunder, will you try to relax and enjoy yourself?'

She nodded slowly, telling herself that Miles was really being very understanding, considering he had guessed she was still attracted to Sebastian. It was a shame to ruin what could be a nice outing. They would both have to work hard again on Monday, whereas every day was a holiday for people like Sebastian.

'All right,' she agreed. 'What would you like me to do, take the helm or set the sails?'

'Neither. You can nip down into the cabin and get us a couple of gins and tonics. We'll drink a toast to our new *entente cordiale.'*

She did as he asked.

Miles' yacht, although well designed, could never have been described as being on the roomy side. It was compact with a long galley that doubled as kitchen, living room and sleeping quarters.

Albany found the drinks where she knew Miles generally kept them. At the same time she stowed the picnic she had prepared into the small fridge. While she did so, she glanced up out of the porthole. They seemed to be sailing at a much faster rate than usual. They were already a long way from land. A small worm of worry crept into her mind but she tried to send it away. Miles had given her his promise to behave. Why should she suddenly doubt him?

She felt her heart lift. Anyway, there was the elderly fisherman she had seen in the harbour, keeping pace with them in spite of his much smaller craft. If she was really in need of help all she had to do was scream at the top of her lungs. It might put Miles off doing something utterly foolish.

Cheerfully she took the drinks up on deck, feeling the wind lift her hair, blowing away some of her troubles. Instantly she felt more carefree.

Miles took the glass she offered and put the wheel on automatic. He slipped his arm through hers companionably.

'That's better. You've decided to make the best of a bad deal. Where would you like to go? There's no reason why we shouldn't go as far as France, if you like. The wind's in our favour. I don't suppose you've brought your passport with you, by any chance?'

'No way,' she laughed. 'We couldn't possibly get there and back in one day.'

He winked. 'Who mentioned one day? We could easily get a friendly French coastguard to telephone your father if you're afraid he'll be worried about you.'

She pulled away from him, suddenly afraid again.

'Don't be silly, Miles!'

'Who's being silly? If you've no passport we could stay aboard.'

She sipped her drink, trying to calm the rising feeling of panic. She had evidently been premature in telling herself Miles was going to behave.

'I think your joke's gone far enough,' she told him tightly.

He finished the last of his drink at a gulp and looked at her over the rim speculatively.

'It's no joke, Albany. A trip to France would be very pleasant. And there are two wide berths in the cabin so you needn't lose any sleep.'

She felt her heartbeat quicken. What a fool she had been to think Miles meant to allow their relationship to remain on a mere friendly footing. And what action could she possibly take if he came on really strong? It would be only her word against his if she reported his behaviour to the Medical Association. It might get into the papers and, even if anyone believed her story, they would think her extremely foolish to have gone sailing with him, knowing he was more attracted to her than she was to him.

Her thoughts were toppling over one another. The gin and tonic didn't help, either. She poured it overboard.

'Hey, no need for that,' Miles said, making a grab to stop her.

'Don't touch me!' she shouted.

'Don't touch you?' he said, narrowing his eyes whilst restraining her in a grip of iron. 'Really, Albany, you're making a mountain out of a molehill. Anyone would think you were fighting for your honour.'

She looked up at him, seeing a small pulse working at the side of his temple. In spite of the amused way he said it, she could see a look behind his blue eyes that terrified her.

'Please let me go,' she pleaded. 'I don't want to go to France. I want to go home — now.'

'Oh, poor little thing,' he said humouring her, 'so she doesn't want to go to France with the big, rough doctor-man. She wants to go home.' His manner hardened. 'Well, let me tell you, Albany, *I* don't want to go back to harbour yet. Not for a long time. So you'd better make up your mind to behave like a big girl and do what big girls do and stop making such a fuss.'

He let go her wrist and thrust her away from him.

'You can go and get me another gin and tonic, and another for yourself just to make up for the one you tipped away. It'll give you a spot of Dutch courage.'

Slowly, she edged away from him, making her way down to the cabin, glad to escape. It was only when she was there, pouring the drinks with her back turned, that she realised it had been a very foolhardy thing to do. She heard Miles' footfall behind at the same moment as the thought struck home. She turned to see him smiling triumphantly down at her, effectively blocking the only way up to the deck, and saw his eyes light on one of the made-up bunks.

'Miles, pull yourself together,' she said, gathering up what bravery she had left. 'Anyone would think you'd gone raving mad. What are you trying to prove, that you're some tough guy on TV?'

He ignored her words, walking slowly towards her.

'You know, you're even more attractive when you're cross. I really don't know how I've managed to keep my hands off you for so long.' His voice was thick with lust.

'You're drunk!' she accused.

'What, on one gin and tonic?'

As he put out his hand to clutch her, she remembered the glass she was holding and hurled the contents in his face. His look of surprise changed to one of anger the moment he surveyed the mess she'd made of his clothes.

'You little wildcat!' he shouted, making a grab for the hand that still held the glass. 'I'll make you pay for that, just see if I don't.'

Then suddenly he had captured her in his sinewy arms, and she knew just what it felt like to be trapped by bands of steel.

'Let me go, Miles!' she screamed. 'Oh, please let me go. This play-acting of yours has gone far enough.'

'It's no pretence,' he assured her harshly. 'Believe me I'm in deadly earnest. So you'd better behave yourself, and start being nice to me. If you don't, you're only going to get hurt.'

She started to sob with fear. 'Please, Miles, don't be such a fool. Just let me go and we'll forget any of this ever happened. How would you feel if I reported you? Surely you don't want to get struck off?'

'No chance of that. I'd only have to tell people you were screaming for it and got cold feet. Who do you think they'd believe, you or me?'

Before she could stop him, he began kissing her passionately. She tried to pull away but his grip was like iron.

184

The next few minutes were like something out of a nightmare. As hard as she tried to escape, he was able to drag her against him again. In the end she felt her strength start to ebb. She was sobbing like a child. She was dimly aware of Miles struggling to get her over to the bunk and she resisted with all her might. In the conflict the thin blouse she was wearing suddenly gave way, exposing her shoulder and part of her breast. The sight of them seemed to inflame Miles' passion even more. She could feel his panting breath scorching her cheek as his hands grappled with the remainder of the blouse, trying to expose more.

'Stop it, oh, stop it!' she screamed. 'Oh, please let me go!'

The cabin door, which had been left partly open, was suddenly kicked wide by a wellingtoned boot, and the fisherman she had seen earlier was standing there. Albany could hardly believe her eyes.

In spite of the hampering oilskins,

the man was able to make a grab for Miles from behind and twist him round to face him with more strength than Albany would have believed an elderly man could possess.

'Right — now let's see how you like a spot of the same rough treatment,' the fisherman told Miles. And it was in that second that Albany recognised Sebastian's voice and thanked God for his goodness.

With a right uppercut, he lifted Miles from the cabin floor and sent him toppling. With another equally fine blow he had the doctor lying flat and stretched out, wondering what had hit him.

The fight was over almost as soon as it had begun. Sebastian flung off his souwester and glanced over at Albany to see if she was all right. She remembered the state she was in and tried to drag the two halves of her flimsy blouse together.

'I shouldn't worry about that,' he said. 'I've seen all there is to see.' He went on more scathingly: 'You'd better decide which boat you're returning in, and make it snappy. I've already wasted nearly half a day on you, I've no intention of wasting more. I'm beginning to wonder whether you're worth the trouble.'

She was filled with gratitude for the way he had turned up out of the blue at the very moment she needed him.

'Yours, Sebastian,' she said in a small voice, 'and thank you for following us.'

He wrinkled up his nose distastefully. 'I wish I could say it had been a pleasure. But if you'd spent as much time in these fish-reeking oilskins as I had, you'd understand my sacrifice.'

He hurled them off, throwing Miles a final look of scorn before preceding Albany up on deck.

She scrambled after him into the rocking dinghy moored alongside before an uncomfortable thought struck her.

'He'll be all right, won't he? I mean Miles. Oughtn't we to make sure he's fully conscious before we leave?'

He looked at her in astonishment.

'You've got a short memory, haven't you?'

She looked back at him miserably. 'I should have taken your advice the other day. You were right, a leopard doesn't change its spots. All the same, I can't help feeling a lot of it was my fault. He must have thought I was fair game.'

He sighed harshly and clambered back on the *Merry Lark*. She watched him go, feeling a tenderness towards him she had never felt for anyone before.

A few moments later he was back. 'He's all right,' he assured her. 'Drinking gin and tonic and smouldering like an angry bison over my treatment of him.' He got back in the dinghy and turned on the motor. 'Let's get going. As I said, I've better things to do with my time than act nursemaid to someone who should know better.'

The journey to shore took longer

in the small craft Sebastian told her he had hired along with the smelly oilskins. Before they were half way there a strong breeze arose, bringing with it a drizzle of rain. The shirt Sebastian had lent her clung to her skin uncomfortably. Albany gave a shiver.

'Are you cold?' he asked with a troubled frown.

'Not really, in shock, I think.' Her teeth chattered together involuntarily.

He grew more concerned. 'Do you think you could bear my arm around you? It'll give you more warmth. I'll get you home the minute I can, and you'll be able to have a hot bath and something warm to drink.'

She found herself gathered tightly against his bare chest. For a moment the thrill of being so close to him took her breath away. Then she murmured: 'I'm all right. I'm only sorry I had to deprive you of your shirt. You must be a lot colder than me.'

She took in what she could see of his tanned, muscular torso, and felt him shrug away her words.

'It's my own fault, I should have brought a coat instead of trying to play Sherlock Holmes in those putrid oilskins.'

She gave a secret smile. The odour of stale fish clung to the shirt she had on but somehow she didn't mind. It was something of his. She would not have rejected it for anything in the world. They were more in tune now, at this moment, than they had been since the night he had unexpectedly kissed her.

The craft made slow progress. There seemed to be something the matter with the outboard motor. The steady drizzle turned into a downpour. Sebastian's dark hair lay in saturated wisps over his forehead, making him even more attractive to her eyes. She was aware that her own hair, which she had piled on top in a thick knot earlier that afternoon, now lay in what felt like a sodden pancake. Odd strands that had escaped in the wind fell in damp, corkscrew curls about her ears.

What a sight I must look, she thought.

The only compensation for the bad weather was that when they finally landed there was no one around to think what an odd pair they looked; Albany half covered in a man's large, wringing wet shirt, and Sebastian, topless in rain-sodden jeans.

He grasped her hand, hurrying her to where he had parked his car out of sight of the harbour in a small back street. No wonder she had missed seeing it earlier!

The journey back to the cottage seemed to take no time at all. In her heart, in spite of the discomfort, Albany wished it had lasted longer. It was heaven to be sitting next to Sebastian, able to study his profile in secret, even though he was probably thinking her the very worst kind of idiot.

When they drove through the drive gates she was relieved to find her father's invalid car nowhere in sight. She had not been looking forward to explaining her condition and the fact that Sebastian had brought her home. She had already made up her mind to tell no one about Miles' behaviour. As he had said, it was her word against his. And, if she made an official complaint it would mean involving Sebastian, and he would probably hate that. Anyway, if she looked at it factually, apart from a few bruises, there had been no actual harm done. The whole thing had been caused in the first place by her ridiculous scheme of trying to make Sebastian jealous. And what had that achieved? He had said hardly anything nice to her since the moment he boarded the *Merry Lark*. He had been full of the fact that she had wasted his precious time without deserving it.

'Well, what are you waiting for?' he asked sharply, interrupting her thoughts. 'Hop out and jump into a hot bath as soon as you can. You're dripping gallons all over my seat.'

She glanced at his expression to see if she could make out the slightest sign of fondness there. But disappointment greeted her. His look was impassive.

She got out as quickly as she could, feeling spurned. 'I'll let you have your shirt back as soon as I've washed it. Thanks again, Sebastian, for saving me from a fate worse than death.'

'You've really only yourself to blame,' he told her callously. 'I warned you about Planter but you refused to listen. Under the circumstances, I thought the least I could do was to be on hand, since I had nothing else to do this afternoon.'

'Oh, spare me the lecture!' she shouted back, suddenly furious with both herself and him. Why give him the satisfaction of thinking she cared a jot for him?

She unlocked the door hastily and slammed it behind her. Then she heard him tear off up the drive.

11

The following morning, none the worse for her ordeal, Albany washed Sebastian's shirt and hung it on the clothes line in the small garden. Her father made only the smallest comment.

'Doing Miles' washing for him now? Can't he afford to send his things to the laundry?'

Albany did not tell him it was Sebastian's. Instead she changed the subject quickly.

'Do I remember you saying something about a committee meeting at your club tonight?'

'Yes, that's right. I've been co-opted on.'

'Isn't Sunday a funny day to have one?'

'Not at all. When you're disabled as well as being unemployed, every day seems much the same. Why, was there something special you'd planned for the two of us this evening?'

'No. If I get a moment I shall go down and see Miss Phipps. She gets lonely now she can't get out so much.'

'Why not see if she'd like to come to some of our club functions?' he suggested. 'I'm sure there'll always be someone happy to collect her and take her home.'

'Thanks, Dad. I'll ask her. She might like that.'

Later that afternoon, Albany ironed Sebastian's shirt, taking a great deal more care over it than she usually gave her own things. While she was doing it, she wondered whether she should use it as an opportunity to see him again. In the end she dismissed it as being too obvious, deciding reluctantly to give it to Rose to take up the next day.

After her father had left for his meeting at eight o'clock, Albany got out her car and went down to the village to see Miss Phipps. The elderly lady was pleased to see her. They spent a pleasant couple of hours together, the old lady relating interesting anecdotes about her youth.

At just after ten, Albany left for home. It was a dark night with the minimum of stars. A crescent moon peeped out once in a while but was hidden more often than not by thick clouds.

When she drove up in front of the cottage she could see her father was not yet home. It seemed likely he was still at his meeting.

She locked her Fiesta away and went up the short path to the front door. It was there that for no known reason her heart began to hammer, and she thought twice about entering the cottage on her own. A sixth sense seemed to tell her something was badly wrong.

As she glanced through the sitting room window she thought she caught the glimmer of a torch, though it might have been the reflection of a car's headlights on the nearby road.

She waited before putting her key in the lock, letting her intuition have its own way. Curious things had happened since they had come to the cottage. She had found out she was extremely sensitive to atmosphere. How else had she known, or felt in her bones, that the woman who had lived there before had been French?

Trying to put the fear of phantoms from her mind, she waited for several long moments, fighting a battle between the realistic side of her nature and the imaginative.

In the end, the realistic side won and she unlocked the door and entered the hall. The moment she did so a scuffling noise from the direction of her father's bedroom told her she was not alone. She felt her hair stand on end.

Reaching out quickly and switching on the hall light, her spirits sank when nothing happened. A wave of hysteria came over her but she quelled it. What a time for the bulb to go!

'Is anyone there?' she cried firmly.

No-one replied. The sitting room led off from the hall and the door was partly open. She stretched out her hand fearfully and tried the other light. Still nothing happened. It was as though all the lights in the cottage had failed.

She remembered she had a small torch in her pocket. Taking it out with trembling fingers she shone it round the sitting room and over to her father's room. No one stirred.

Shining the torch around, one of the first things she noticed was that the beautiful crystal vase was no longer in its place. Ever since he had bought it, Sebastian had made sure Jefferson kept it filled with roses. She saw them now, lying strewn about the carpet. Then she felt the crunch of glass beneath her feet. A further inspection told her the vase lay shattered in thousands of shards. She drew in her breath sharply. How had such a thing happened?

Her question was answered in the next second. A figure darted out from a dark corner, knocking her and the torch flying. Albany heard the intruder escaping through the front door. Recovering herself quickly she made to follow. As though on cue, the moon came out and she could see clearly that the person was a woman. Thin as a young boy, dressed in dark jeans and a jumper, the woman had the grace of a gazelle. Her long, dark hair fanned out like a cloud behind her as she ran.

For a moment Albany almost gave up the chase before it began. The woman was far too fleet for her. Then she saw her trip and fall. It was the chance she needed. Why should the woman make off with whatever she had stolen without some effort on Albany's part?

Without thinking whether the woman may be armed, Albany tore after her. She reached her just as she was getting to her feet. For a moment the woman faced her. With the moon shining down Albany had a clear view of her features. Although she couldn't remember having met her before, there was something very familiar about her. She realised what it was the moment the woman spoke.

'I have stolen nothing. If you know what's good for you you'll forget you ever saw me. Go back to the cottage. I have no quarrel with you!'

With the agility of an athlete, the woman turned and made off again. Albany stood looking after her, too surprised and shocked to give chase again.

A few seconds after the woman had reached the drive gates she heard the sound of a car start up and speed away swiftly. Feeling dazed and bewildered, Albany made her way slowly back to the cottage.

Her brain was in a whirl. The woman couldn't possibly be the person she thought she was. It was impossible. The last tenant of the cottage, Corinne

Latour, was dead — drowned at Hunters Cove. Yet the intruder's features had been exactly the same as those in the photograph. It was possible, too, it had been the same person she had observed in the drive the night she had burnt it. What's more, the woman had a strong French accent!

As Albany entered the cottage she suddenly remembered about the lights. If, by some remote chance, the woman she had seen tonight *was* Corinne, and she hadn't drowned that day as everyone in the vicinity thought, then she would probably have had a key to the front door. Also, since she had lived there, she would have known where the fuse boxes were located. It was too much of a coincidence to think the lights had conveniently failed on their own.

She fumbled her way to where they were, high up on the kitchen wall. Then she felt for the box of matches she kept there in case of emergency, breathing a sigh of relief when she found them. Striking a match, she saw at once that the trip switch had been thrown. She moved it back to its normal position. At once the lights that had been left on in the hall and sitting room burst into life.

She made a quick survey of the cottage. The only thing that seemed out of place was the beautiful crystal vase and its contents. She cleared up the mess of water and broken flowers, getting out the hoover to gather up the thousands of pieces of glass.

Her father came home while she was doing it. He wheeled his chair into the sitting room and exclaimed: 'Cleaning up at this time of night! I thought Rose came on Mondays.'

'She does. I've had an accident. I can't leave it for her.'

Albany had already decided not to tell her father about the intruder. There was no point in worrying him. She saw him glance over to where the vase usually stood in all its glory.

'Oh, Lord — not that crystal thing?'

'Afraid so. I knocked against it when I was putting some of my physio equipment in the cupboard underneath.'

She thought the small fabrication well worth his peace of mind.

'Sebastian will have to be told,' he murmured.

'Of course. I shall do that tomorrow.' She put on a yawn. 'If you don't mind, I'm going to bed now. Incidentally, *you're* home late. I thought most meetings ended about ten.'

He gave a smile. 'They do, unless they're held in the back room of the Petersville Arms.'

She raised an eyebrow. 'I hope you're not drinking and driving!'

He laughed. 'A half of cider is my limit, I promise.'

She kissed him goodnight and went up the stairs.

Although Albany was weary, sleep didn't come easily. Her mind was too full of the events of the evening. If it had not been for the broken vase she would have thought she had imagined the whole thing. The longer she thought about it the more fantastic it became. The beautiful French woman alive when everyone had presumed her dead! And what had she been doing in the cottage? How had she come to break the vase? Why had she not interfered with anything else?

It was well after two in the morning when she finally fell asleep, thinking uneasily that if the woman still had a key she could come back any time she liked. Oh, why, why wasn't life simple like it had once been? Why did her mother's tragic death and her father's paralysis have to turn her once-orderly life into a tangle of problems and torments?

She woke in the morning to the sight of bright sunshine streaming into the room. Everything appeared so normal she thought she had had a bad dream, until she went downstairs and saw at once the empty place where the crystal vase had been.

Later that day she knew she would have to go up and see Sebastian. Although she dreaded the ordeal, her heart thrilled at the thought of seeing him. Apart from telling him about the breakage, it would be necessary to brave his wrath and tell him she suspected the French woman was still alive. What would his reaction be to that, she wondered?

On her way home at lunchtime, instead of stopping directly at the cottage, she drove on up the drive, parking her car next to Sebastian's Porsche in the Manor's forecourt.

He heard her drive up and opened the front door while she was still getting out.

'Come in! To what do I owe this pleasure?'

He studied her as she came towards him, still dressed in her white overall, nipped in at the waist with the large belt that she always wore when she was working.

'It looks as though it's important.

Have you come straight from work?'

She nodded. 'Yes, and it is.'

He gave her a questioning look and she decided to dive right in. Taking a deep breath, she told him: 'I'm afraid your lovely crystal vase is no more. It's been broken. I'm dreadfully sorry.'

His face broke into a smile. 'Is that all? I thought it was something much more important. I'll buy you another to replace it.'

She couldn't resist her slightly tart reply. 'What it is to be rich — money no object!'

'Would you like to come in?' he asked, ignoring the comment. 'Or are you in a hurry?'

'No, I'm not in a hurry. And there's something more, Sebastian.'

He studied her anxious look when she was sitting opposite him in the sitting room.

'Can I get you a drink?'

She shook her head. 'No, thanks.'

'Fire away then,' he said.

He watched her as she tried to gather

her thoughts together and put them into words. It was curious how his need of her seemed to grow with each day. Even the first time they had met, in spite of their disagreement, he had found her infinitely desirable. Every night she haunted his dreams, as no one else had since his love affair with Corinne. During the last year he had begun to think he was immune to women, but Albany had shattered all that.

'It's difficult to know where to start,' she said.

'It's always as well to try the beginning. Has it anything to do with the broken vase?'

'Everything.'

'How did it happen?'

She shook her head. 'I've no idea. It wasn't me that broke it, you see. It was already done when I got home last night . . .'

He tried to take in what she was telling him, in spite of the frustrating things she was doing to his heart. For once her blue eyes were immensely serious. The sunlight streaming in behind turned her fair hair into a halo. She had a madonna look about her.

'. . . I had a feeling someone was in there even before I opened the door. Then I heard a noise, and the lights wouldn't go on. I switched on my torch and saw the vase, or rather the shattered pieces. Then someone came bursting through from somewhere and knocked me flying!'

'You weren't hurt in any way?'

His solicitude touched her. Why hadn't he shown the same concern when he had saved her from Miles?

She gave a little shrug. 'No, they weren't as rough as all that. Actually, it was a woman.'

She waited for his reaction. None showed, unless it was a slight look of puzzlement.

'A woman! That's rather unusual. One always has the impression most burglars are men.'

'I don't think this one was a real

burglar. In fact, the more I think about it, the more I feel they were probably searching for something.'

'Like what?'

'I don't know,' she said slowly. 'I was hoping you might be able to throw some light on it.'

'Why should you think that?'

She summoned up her courage. 'Because — I'm sorry if this comes as a shock to you — but the woman, I feel sure, was Corinne Latour!'

He gave a harsh gasp of surprise.

'How do you know what Corinne looks like? Had you met her, by any chance?'

'No, never. But I found her photograph, if you remember, the one you told me to burn. And the woman last night had a French accent.'

'You heard this person speak? What did she say?'

Albany did not have to think about it. The words had been with her since the woman had uttered them.

'She said: *I have stolen nothing. If*

you know what's good for you you'll forget you ever saw me. Go back to the cottage. I have no quarrel with you.'

Without making any comment, Sebastian went over to where he kept the drinks and poured himself a scotch.

'Will you change your mind?' he asked.

'No thank you.'

He came back with his drink and sat down, nursing it without speaking. The silence became deafening. Albany felt she had to break it.

'It's not the first time I've seen her. She was there, looking in the window the night you asked me to burn her photo. At first I thought she was a ghost. I've felt her presence ever since the first day we came. I knew she was French before I was even told. I've often had the feeling I'm psychic. But last night, I knew for certain the woman was real. Ghosts don't push people out of the way, they don't stop and talk to you when they're cornered, and they certainly don't wear expensive

French perfume!'

Sebastian nodded. 'No, no, of course not. And you're right — ' he looked out of the window thoughtfully — 'the intruder *was* Corinne, it had to be. I've always known, deep at the bottom of my heart, that one day she'd come back.'

Albany studied his expression. He looked sad and drawn as though he had just got over a serious illness. She felt her heart go out to him. What had gone wrong between him and the French girl? Surely Sebastian should have been the first person Corinne went to, to let him know she was alive? She tried to feel glad for him that the love he had thought dead had returned, but only succeeded in feeling sorry for herself.

'I'd better go,' she said, standing up. 'Father will be wanting his lunch.'

Sebastian put his drink down, still untouched, and got up, too.

'It's time I told you the truth,' he said quietly, 'that is, if you're interested enough to hear it.'

12

Albany sat down again. She had a feeling that what was to come would astonish her. But she was unprepared for Sebastian's next statement.

'You see,' he said, turning his back on her and going over to stare out of the window, 'I've known ever since the day it happened that Corinne was still alive.'

Albany gave a little gasp. Sebastian went straight on.

'As you probably know, Corinne was living at the cottage when I took over the Manor. The first time I saw her I became deeply infatuated. I wasn't the only person. As I found out later I was just one of many. Corinne couldn't live without the company of men. She welcomed my attentions as much as she welcomed everyone else's. In a fit of moon madness one evening I asked her to marry me. She laughed in my face. I demanded to know what was so funny and she told me. She was married already, she said. The information came as an incredible surprise. For some reason, she confided in me more than she'd confided in anyone else living in the village. Her husband, she told me, was serving a prison sentence for drug offences. The moment he came out she'd be on her way again.'

He stopped and came back and sat down. Albany waited for him to continue.

'I thought I might learn to despise her after what she'd said. A married woman who goes out with other men is a distasteful creature. But Corinne had a fascination few people possess, and she was really extremely beautiful.'

Albany felt she would scream if anyone mentioned the French woman's beauty again. She couldn't resist a slightly catty remark.

'I'm afraid I didn't notice her beauty

last night. To me she seemed over-thin. But I'm much more interested to know what happened at Hunters Cove. If everyone else thought she had drowned, how was it you knew she was still alive?'

He sighed. 'It's not difficult to stage a drowning. It was about a month after she'd told me about herself. I'd tried not to see her so often. But that day I followed her. It was quite early in the morning. She occasionally went off for an early morning swim. I followed her across the fields at a distance. Don't ask me why, I don't really remember. I only know I felt a deep anger and resentment burning inside. It was probably jealousy. I watched her strip down to her bikini and walk into the sea. For the first time, I noticed a boat out there — a small yacht similar to Miles'. I thought it *was* his at first. Then I realised it was more streamlined. She started to swim out towards it. It was some way from the shore but she was a strong swimmer. After she reached it, it was an easy job for the person aboard to haul her over the side. I wondered about all the subterfuge if she was simply meeting another man. She was never so secretive about all her other affairs. And then the yacht's motor started up and it headed out to sea. I waited around for several hours but it didn't put in another appearance. Later someone found her clothes on the beach and the rumour got around that she'd drowned.'

Albany was amazed. 'But surely you scotched that rumour at once?'

He shook his head. 'I'm afraid I didn't. Any rate, later it was taken out of my hands.'

'In what way?'

'Naturally I went to see the police eventually. I told them what I'd seen. They informed me in confidence that Corinne's husband had absconded the day before. It seemed more than likely, they said, that he was on board the yacht I'd seen and they'd both sailed over to France. As it happens, that's exactly what occurred. They were both arrested by Interpol. The last I heard before I left England was that they were serving prison sentences over there.'

Albany looked at him. 'You never told anyone else in the village the truth?'

He shrugged. 'Why should I? I left the country very soon after the incident. If the police and the press thought fit to kill the story why should I make it my business to shout the truth around?'

She got up. 'Thank you for telling me what happened, Sebastian. I appreciate your confidence.' Her voice sounded stilted to her. She hoped he would not guess she was smouldering with jealousy.

He accompanied her to the door. 'I'll get Jefferson or someone to change the locks at the cottage. It seems certain Corinne still has a key. It's possible she may come back again now she's out of prison.'

'But why? What is there in the

cottage? Your step-mother had every trace of the last tenant removed, except for her photograph. And she'd hardly be likely to come back for that.'

He looked down at her thoughtfully. 'I don't know. All the same, I'll have the locks changed. I don't want to risk danger to you in any way.'

For the first time she saw an odd look of tenderness in his gaze. It prompted a spontaneous invitation from her.

'Are you doing anything special this evening? It's father's birthday. I shall be preparing dinner for us at eight, if you'd like to come.'

She felt her heart rise in her throat as she waited for his reply. When it came it brought disappointment although his refusal sounded sad.

'There's really nothing I'd have liked better, but I have a prior engagement. Believe me when I say it's not the kind one can easily get out of. It would mean letting too many people down.'

'Don't bother to apologise,' she interrupted, feeling hurt and let-down.

She hurried over to her car and drove off without giving him a backward glance.

★ ★ ★

All through that evening she tried to cast sadness away, pretending a brightness she didn't feel. She refused to spoil her father's birthday for anything. The feeble excuse Sebastian had made still rankled. Why on earth couldn't he have told the truth: that that sort of evening would bore him to tears!

For the birthday meal she'd spared no expense. On her way home that morning she had purchased a brace of grouse and all the trimmings to go with them. Although no great chef, she'd prepared them in the afternoon, ready for the evening meal.

They were pronounced an enormous success by her father, who lingered over their flavour before accepting a portion of the sweet she had made.

'This one's a bit of cheat,' she told him, placing an attractive looking concoction before him. 'It's mainly ice-cream. I didn't think you'd want anything too heavy after all that.'

He agreed. 'There was really far too much for two. I bet you've got stacks left over. We should have invited someone else to share it with us.'

She kept her back turned to him on purpose as she collected up some of the used dishes.

'I asked Sebastian, but it seems he had what's politely known as a *prior engagement.*'

Darrel was quick to sense her disbelief.

'It's quite possible he was telling the truth,' he said softly. 'He doesn't seem the type to turn down a pretty woman's invitation out of hand.'

'No, well, thanks for the compliment. I expect he saw the evening as an utter bore after all the luxury he must be used to.'

Her father gave a hearty laugh.

'Don't fool yourself. Sebastian Blaire can't keep his eyes off you. I've known it for some while. He watches you a great deal from a distance. You've either not been aware, or else you're too modest to admit it. I shouldn't brush off his *prior engagement* too lightly.'

Albany escaped to the kitchen quickly, feeling her face turning fiery. Was her father telling the truth? Did Sebastian really keep a look-out for her from the Manor without her knowing? Was his sarcastic behaviour towards her just an act? Did he really think more of her than she guessed? A shudder of desire ran through her. If she could only believe that, and give herself hope.

She came back to earth, eyeing the enormous amount of washing up she had made for herself. She decided to do something she rarely did, and leave it for the morning since she had no early appointments.

She heard her father switch the television on. He had mentioned earlier that there was a programme he wanted to see. She got back into the sitting room just as the credits were being shown and the opening music played.

They settled down to watch it together. It was a programme about much needed aid for the African states. Albany felt herself growing emotionally involved as pictures of the famine and desolation came onto the small screen, and mothers with small babies in their arms stared dejectedly into the cameras.

At the end of the short film, the presenter announced that the organiser of a well-known relief fund was in the studio, ready to answer questions about his work.

It was then Albany received a shock even greater than the one she had suffered the night before. There, before her eyes, looking slightly smarter than he usually did, was Sebastian. She felt herself go hot and cold. He was wearing a smart grey suit and his hair looked neatly brushed. He appeared completely at home in the interviewer's comfortable leather chair.

She was too surprised even to gasp. They both remained silent, listening raptly to the presenter's questions and Sebastian's intelligent answers.

Later another short film was shown which included him. He was looking far less smart, but infinitely more workmanlike, in crumpled shorts and a safari hat. Albany imagined the discomfort he must have felt, braving the fierce sun, the flies, the smell of the disease ridden camps, all to see for himself the plight of the people he was working for.

At the end, after an appeal had been made for more funds and Sebastian had disappeared from the screen, she put a hand up, covering her expression from her father's gaze.

'I feel so ashamed,' she confessed in a small voice. 'That I should have had the audacity to think Sebastian was telling lies, when all the time he knew he was going to be on television and hadn't told a soul.'

'Not quite. He told me when I saw him in the drive just as he was about to set off for London. He wished me a happy birthday, then asked me to respect his confidence.'

She looked at him accusingly. 'So you knew all the time he was going to be on the television?'

'That's so. If you remember, I warned you not to dismiss his refusal so lightly.'

She was filled with remorse. 'To think of all the times I've thrown his idleness up at him, when actually he was working harder than any of us, not only organising everything, but going out there, seeing for himself the ordeal and suffering, being amongst the dead and the dying and doing his best to get relief for them!'

A sob escaped her. Her father put out a hand and stroked her hair.

'Don't be too hard on yourself, Albany. We all make mistakes sometimes.'

'But I was so scathing! So sanctimonious!'

'If you feel as badly as that, you could always make it the excuse to go up and apologise, and tell him how much we admire the work he's doing.'

She nodded, looking into the distance. It would take a lot of courage to apologise to Sebastian and tell him how wrong she had been about him. That was the trouble with having so much pride.

But, she consoled herself, if her father was right about Sebastian's secret regard for her, perhaps it wouldn't be too hard.

13

The opportunity for Albany to go up and see Sebastian did not occur until fairly late the following evening. The director of the local hospital had rung her first thing in the morning to ask if she would take the place of their usual physiotherapist who had fallen ill. It would have been difficult to refuse, although it had meant altering the times of most of her private patients' appointments.

At nine in the evening she began her walk up to the Manor. Dusk was coming in. It had been a fine September day. The summer warmth still showed no signs of fading and had amply made up for the violent storms of the winter.

It was only as she neared the large house that her courage began to fail. Supposing her father had mis-read the signs of Sebastian's regard for her? What if he had made it up, thinking to please her? It would look as though she were throwing herself at him, going up at this time of night. He would wonder why she couldn't have come during the day.

She was about to return and think the situation out again when she heard footsteps on the gravel some way behind, and looked over her shoulder uneasily.

It was difficult to see anything in the poor light, but it was clear someone else, like her, was making their way up to the Manor. And the footsteps didn't sound as though they belonged to a man.

Acting on impulse, she left the path quickly and squeezed herself between the thick fir trees that bordered the drive. They served as an excellent hiding place. She remained there silent, hardly daring to breathe, hoping she might be able to identify the other person as she passed.

She didn't have long to wait. Within moments a woman had caught her up and walked by. Albany had no difficulty, at such short range, in recognising her as the person who had threatened her in the drive two nights before. She felt her pulse quicken. She waited several moments more, wondering whether she should follow the woman up to the Manor. Had Corinne perhaps telephoned Sebastian to let him know she was coming, or was it a surprise visit? Would he welcome her arrival? Was he still infatuated, even after everything that had happened?

She decided eventually to go up without announcing her presence too loudly. It was just possible that Corinne intended, for some reason, to break into the Manor as unlawfully as she had entered the cottage. After all, she would not be aware that Sebastian knew she was still alive, if she had left her clothes on the beach that day intentionally in order to let people think she had drowned.

Albany traversed the rest of the way as quietly as she could, walking along the grass verge where her footsteps were muffled. When she reached the paved forecourt in front of the Manor, she took off her shoes and carried them in her hand, going silently over to the sitting room window where she could hear voices drifting out.

The curtains looked as though they had been hurriedly drawn. Large gaps showed between them where the light shone through. The windows, due to the fine weather, had been left wide open.

Hating herself for playing the sordid role of eaves-dropper, Albany stayed to listen. The French woman's voice with its lilting accent floated to her on the still air.

' . . . a year, my dear Sebastian, yes, I know, a whole year, and don't think I haven't frequently ached to write to you and tell you the whole truth!'

'But still you allowed me and others

to believe you'd drowned!'

'Yes, it was unforgivable, but entirely necessary — or so I thought at the time.'

'How could you be so unfeeling?'

'It wasn't easy, but, then, neither is a year spent in prison for aiding and abetting my husband to escape.'

'Where is he now?'

'Still there — and I hope he rots for all the grief he has given me!' Her tone sounded vehement.

A moment or two passed before Sebastian replied. His voice sounded softer.

'Why have you returned?'

Corinne's voice became seductive.

'Can't you guess? It was always you I wanted, Sebastian, deep in my heart. I pretended to spurn you, simply because I knew my husband intended to escape. I found out his friends were watching me. I couldn't get out of going back to France with him, but I didn't want to drag you into it as well. I knew there would be another time, a time when

I was free of him, when we could be together!'

Albany felt her heart drop. She didn't want to wait to hear Sebastian's reply. She had heard enough to know she had lost. Whatever he had told her about Corinne would now be null and void. She had come back and was offering herself on a plate to him. How could he resist her?

Then a sharp sound behind alerted her. Out of the corner of her eye she caught sight of a man. His arm was raised and in his clenched fist she could see something that looked hard and shiny. His purpose was obvious.

'No, oh, no!' she cried, trying to ward off the blow. But something landed with a thud on the side of her head and she dropped to the ground like a stone.

★ ★ ★

Later on it was never entirely clear to Albany how long she remained unconscious. After falling in a heap at the bottom of the front door steps, the next thing she knew she was on the couch in Sebastian's sitting room. Her head seemed to be resting in someone's lap. Focussing her eyes with difficulty, she could see Corinne was still there. She was standing next to a man who was holding a revolver and pointing it roughly in the direction of the couch. Corinne and the man were arguing fiercely. The man had a London accent. He looked thin, barely more than a youth and very scruffy.

' 'ow was I to know you'd got things under control? I came up to see 'ow things were goin' and I saw 'er there, listening to everything you and 'im were saying. I did the first thing that came into me head and 'it her one!'

'You've ruined everything, you stupid, lumbering moron!'

' 'ere — 'oo are you callin' names?'

'You, you filthy imbecile!'

'I don't take that, comin' from a French jailbird like you!'

231

'Oh, let's stop calling each other names. The harm's done. Help me to find the vase. It's got to be here somewhere. It wasn't in the cottage.'

'Wot's it look like?'

'It's blue, a large, blue pottery vase!' She turned on Sebastian, who Albany had just realised was the person holding her head gently in his lap and stroking her forehead. 'Where is it? What have you done with it?' The French woman's eyes narrowed menacingly. 'If you don't tell me, I shall ask Lonnie to kill you both. He's itching to try out the new toy I've bought him.'

'Stop being melodramatic, Corinne. That's the type of thing they were saying in American gangster films before you were born.'

Between her eyelashes, Albany watched her stalk dangerously towards them. Then she heard the sound of a slap and felt Sebastian flinch.

'Keep your comments to yourself. Just tell me what you have done with that vase! Why did you remove it from the cottage and put that revolting crystal one in its place?'

'Wasn't it to your liking?' Sebastian said in a scathing tone. 'Is that the reason you smashed it?'

'How did you know that? Did *she* tell you? In that case my visit to you tonight was no surprise!'

There was a moment's silence. Albany wanted to groan, her bump on the head was hurting. But she wasn't sure it was wise to let Corinne and the man who had coshed her know she was conscious. Besides, even though she was in pain, it was soothing to feel Sebastian's tender touch and the warmth of his body close to her.

She heard him give a sigh. 'No, you're quite right. I had a feeling you'd be here before long. I puzzled things out. It had to be the blue vase you were searching for. And I soon found out the reason.'

The next moment everything seemed to happen in a rush, like the speeding up of a video. The curtains suddenly parted and several men in police uniform jumped through. The youth's gun went off like a clap of thunder. Albany screamed and sat up in time to see Corinne struggling and kicking in the grip of two of the men. But Sebastian took no notice of what was going on around. All his attention was focussed on Albany.

'Oh, my darling, if only I could have saved you this. How are you feeling? What a hell of a time you chose to come visiting.'

She stared at him, confused for a second because he had called her darling. But there was no mistaking the tenderness in his gaze.

'I — I don't understand,' she said in a bewildered manner.

'You will. I promise you I'll explain later. But it's important to get you to a hospital first and find out whether you've got any concussion from that blow you were dealt.'

He helped her to her feet. Corinne and the youth were being hustled noisily out of the house. Sebastian had a few words with the policeman who seemed to be in charge. Then, when everyone had left, he led her gently out to his car.

★ ★ ★

The examination at the local hospital proved Sebastian's fears well founded. Albany had suffered some concussion from the bash on the head she had received. It was not until several days later that she was able to take in all Sebastian had to tell her.

It was late afternoon and he had just finished walking her slowly around the rose garden. Jefferson was just leaving after finishing off his dead-heading.

'Let's sit down,' Sebastian suggested, steering her towards an arbour where climbing pink floribundas formed a canopy over a rustic bench.

Albany sat down gratefully. She was still finding the events that had happened difficult to believe.

'So Corinne was really the main person involved in the drug offences and not her husband?'

Sebastian nodded. 'Yes, it appears so. She allowed her husband to serve the prison sentence in England instead of her. And then carried on her awful trade, involving anyone else she thought fit, usually seeing they were well hooked beforehand.'

'But why did she agree to go back to France with him when her husband escaped, pretending to have drowned?'

'That was all a mistake. She had no intention of going back to France. She was already wanted for several minor offences there unconnected with drugs. When she swam out to the yacht she thought she was collecting her usual supplies. She'd no idea her husband would be on board. He'd heard from other people about the good time she was leading, allowing everyone to think she was single, and decided to put a stop to it. Even if it meant getting re-caught and having his sentence lengthened.'

'So that morning she left the cottage early she'd no idea she wouldn't be returning later?'

'None at all. If she had, she certainly wouldn't have left all that money and her supplies of heroin in the secret base she'd made in the blue vase.'

Albany nodded. 'I think I understand it all now. The vase was still in the cottage the first time I looked round. I suppose Olivia took a fancy to it herself and had it brought up to the Manor. Then, when I told you about Corinne being in the cottage when father and I were out, and breaking the crystal vase, you examined the blue one on a hunch and found out what it contained.'

He humoured her gently. 'What a clever little detective you are.'

She looked up at him. 'But not clever enough to realise someone like you couldn't be idle. I came up that night to apologise and to tell you how much I admired the worthwhile work you were doing.'

He coloured slightly. 'That's kind of you.'

'No,' she said, tracing the tiny lines of character that showed under his eyes beneath the sun tan. 'It's big of *you*.'

And then she was in his arms and for the first time he was telling her how much he loved her. She could not really believe it, although her heart felt it would burst with so much happiness. The fact that Sebastian could return the love she felt for him seemed as incredible as everything else that had happened.

'I knew the moment you told me Corinne had pushed you aside how very much you meant to me,' he murmured. 'Everything I'd ever felt for her died in that moment. When I found what the vase contained it was no torment to me to inform the police. They kept the Manor under surveillance from a distance. But they weren't quick enough to prevent you getting hurt. When I ran out and found what that idiot boy had done to you I thought I'd die.'

'It was *you* who carried me in then?'

'Who else? If you only knew the torment I went through in those few moments. I'm still thinking of bringing a case against the police for not arriving sooner and inadvertently putting your life in danger.'

'Oh, please don't let's talk about it any more.'

'You're right,' he said, putting her away from him slightly and examining her eyes that mirrored his. 'We have so many wonderful things to talk about.' With one hand he felt in his pocket and brought out a small box. Smiling secretly, he handed it to her. 'Open this, Albany. I bought it earlier today in the hope that you'd accept it.'

'What is it?' she whispered, knowing full well but hardly daring to hope.

'Open it and see.'

She did so, giving a small gasp at the sight of such a large diamond set in a gold engagement ring.

'Do you think it will fit you? Put it on,' he pleaded.

A little of the old Albany showed through as she replied flippantly:

'It really depends what it's for, Sebastian. I mean, if it's just for all the trouble I've been through with this ex girl-friend of yours roughing me up, and her new boy-friend knocking me about, I think it's far too expensive for a get-well present!'

He laughed. Then he became serious, his dark eyes gazing at her lovingly.

'Look at me, Albany, and tell me what you see! Do you see someone who is capable of taking care of you for the rest of your days? Someone who will cherish and adore you till the end of time? Who will never be content unless you're by his side? Who is not very good at telling you how much he worships you, but who will do it every day of his life if only you will let him?' He paused, studying her steadfast blue eyes deeply. 'Because, if you do, my dearest Albany, you will put my ring on, or let me do so for you, and then tell me in return you love me as much as I love you.'

Suddenly it seemed to be the easiest and most delightful thing she had ever been asked to do in all her life. And in that same moment, she knew that however old she grew to be, and in whatever drought-ridden, desolate country Sebastian took her to for his work's sake, the scent of roses in an English garden would always bring back this memory.

'I love you, Sebastian. I have since I met you, and I always will.'

She raised her lips for him to take, and the kisses he rained down on them were like summer dew on a parched meadow.

THE END